Glitter

A Babygirl Drama

Glitter

A Babygirl Drama

Babygirl Daniels

www.urbanbooks.net

Urban Books, LLC
1199 Straight Path
West Babylon, NY 11704

ISBN-13: 978-1-60162-198-6
ISBN- 10: 1-60162-198-1

First Printing December 2009
Printed in the United States of America

10 9 8 7 6 5 4 3 2 1

Distributed by Kensington Publishing Corp.
Submit Wholesale Orders to:
Kensington Publishing Corp.
C/O Penguin Group (USA) Inc.
Attention: Order Processing
405 Murray Hill Parkway
East Rutherford, NJ 07073-2316
Phone: 1-800-526-0275
Fax: 1-800-227-9604

Prologue

Ms. Coleman, my high school counselor, sat behind her desk and stared silently at me. I could feel her eyes burning a hole through me. Her stare was filled with concern. I was afraid and did not know whether or not my secret would be safe with her. I did not want anyone to find out what I was hiding, what I had been going through these last couple of months. After all, what would they think of me if they knew? Surely my aunt Joy, the woman who sacrificed and took me in after my father was murdered, would be mad at me. My friends would probably be too through with me and desert me. I can see all of my teachers now looking down on me.

Once I admitted the truth, I knew what my fate

would be. I wished that I could rewind time to take back all of the wrongdoings that littered my history. I would go back and make different decisions, better decisions. I certainly wouldn't brush off all of the advice that my aunt had tried to give me all along. Instead, I would embrace her words of wisdom and not just let my aunt's lessons go in one ear and out the other. I would definitely appreciate her. I would respect her and take her words to heart. Now it was too late though. Even though I loved my aunt dearly, she was the last person I wanted to go to in order to help me out with the bad way I was now in.

My high school counselor seemed to be the only person I had to turn to. I knew that I had to tell someone, because the burden I was carrying was too heavy to bear on my own. I was too young to have been given the burden in the first place. That sounds ironic coming from me, considering I thought I was grown. In actuality I was not. I was a little girl who was stuck between a rock and a hard place. Now I felt as though Ms. Coleman was my last hope, my only option.

"What brings you into my office today, Asia?" Ms. Coleman asked as she attempted to straighten the mess of papers that was spread across the top of her desk.

I played with my fingers while looking down at my hands as the butterflies in my stomach caused me to become nauseous. I couldn't even bring myself to look up. I did not want to look into the eyes of my counselor, the woman who I felt always respected me no matter what others said about me. But that's just how Ms. Coleman was. She wasn't like other adults who demanded respect just because they were an elder. She showed respect and therefore earned it back. That's why she got along well with every student at school. She was smart like that and knew her way around kids. Not just kids, but teenage kids, and anybody who knows anything about teenagers knows that we are not the easiest bunch to befriend.

Ms. Coleman was wise beyond her years, too wise at times. As a matter of fact, knowing Ms. Coleman, if I was to look up at her, she'd probably be able to see right through me. She would be able to read me from cover to cover, like I was her favorite book, before I even began to confide in her what was on page one. That's just how she was. The kids at my high school couldn't put anything past

Ms. Coleman, which was probably why the school system hired her in the first place. She could get through to all the kids, have 'em confessing sins like she was a Catholic priest or something. And she was so good, that often times she knew the sin even before it was confessed, or on good days, before it was even committed.

"Don't you go hanging out with them fools drinking and getting high," she'd warn a few students as they fled the building after school had let out. "I don't want to see you in my office for not turning in your project that's due tomorrow, so cut that television off tonight and get to work," she'd say to others. "I don't care if it is the season finale of *American Idol.*"

I mean, this woman was so good that one time this white chick named Theta was simply walking down the hall and Ms. Coleman pulled her to the side and asked her to come into her office so she could talk to her in private. Theta's bottom barely hit the chair before Ms. Coleman outright asked her, "How long have you had it and have you been to see a doctor?"

Theta burst out crying. Thanks to the bionic ears of Sonya, a junior who worked in the office and happened to hear everything that was being said, before Theta even walked out of Ms. Coleman's office the entire school knew that Theta had caught herpes from her boyfriend, Jason.

Now here I sat, just as Theta had, only my problem was different. When I saw Ms. Coleman standing outside her office greeting students, I almost turned around and went another way. I figured she sensed something was up with me just by looking at me. That is why I'd gripped my school books for dear life, looked straight down and tried to make a bee line to my next class. But in all honesty, when I heard her call out my name, I felt a sense of relief. I had already made it up in my mind that it was time to confide in someone. That someone had just happened to have been Ms. Coleman, only I still needed to juice myself up with courage. I would have avoided her if she hadn't called out to me, but since she did, there was no need in putting it off. I needed someone to confide in, and Ms. Coleman was the only one I could turn to.

Just sitting here in Ms. Coleman's office thinking about the mess I was now caught up in made me sick to my stomach. I could taste the vomit in the back of my throat, and a few beads of sweat formed on my forehead. It felt like the heat had been turned up to sweltering and I shifted uncomfortably in my seat. Tears built in my eyes and I wiped them away quickly. Sitting here gave a new meaning to sitting in the hot seat.

"Asia? What's wrong? Are you okay?" The concern that Ms. Coleman displayed in her tone of voice was the exact reason why I had decided to tell her the secret I held.

Ms. Coleman was cool with all of the students at Cass High. At only 27 years of age, she was the youngest teacher in the school. When she had introduced herself on the first day of school she told us about how she'd graduated high school at only sixteen and a half, went on to college from there, and how she'd been in the school system every since graduating college. She was so inspiring. Almost all the girls at Cass High wanted to be like her. Of course all the boys wanted to date her. Ms. Coleman was cool like that. She always made it a point to speak to the students whenever she saw us in the halls. She even invited us to have lunch in her office whenever we felt like it. I was comfortable around her. I respected her and I trusted her more than any other adult that I knew.

"I need help, Ms. Coleman," I finally replied. My usually confident swagger was reduced by insecurity and fear of the unknown.

"What's going on?" Ms. Coleman replied with her usual vibrancy and Colgate smile. This was her attempt to not look so worried, but the same way she had probably already peeped my game, I had peeped hers. She was a genuine counselor, and she was genuinely concerned. She had a motherly aura about her, yet she was still young enough to understand me. That is why I looked up to her so much. She wasn't stuffy like most adults, but laid back and chill. Anytime I had ever gone to Ms. Coleman about things that were going on in my life, she had never judged me. Instead she listened with an open ear, mind, and heart. She was so cool that I would have hung out with her after school.

"I'm in trouble," I admitted. I became emotional and my words stumbled out of my mouth clumsily as my emotions tried to reveal themselves. I choked up as water built in my eyes.

Ms. Coleman frowned and put up a finger. "Hold on, sweetheart," she said. She stood and walked over to her office door then closed it, flipping the lock as well. "It looks like this is serious. We need a little bit of privacy." I guess she learned to be more discreet after the Theta incident. Ms. Coleman sat back down in her chair and continued. "Now what's on your mind, Asia? I'm listening."

"I'm pregnant," I blurted out as a tear trail blazed down my dark chocolate cheeks. It felt so good to just say those words, like some of the weight had been lifted off of my shoulders. It was as if now that I had admitted it to someone else, I was admitting it to myself. I doubled over in petite sobs and buried my face in my hands. How could I have been so stupid to get caught up like this?

"Oh, Asia," Ms. Coleman sympathized as she stood and walked around to kneel beside my chair. Her comforting hand rubbed my back as she allowed me to release everything I felt inside. "Let it out, sweetheart. Cry your heart out. When you are done, I will help you. We will discuss your options."

Unable to speak and with knots invading the pit of my stomach, I cried relentlessly. I cried so hard that my sobs became heaves of dry air and then finally there was nothing left. I had emptied out my soul right there in my counselor's office. Now I was left with confusion, red eyes, and despair. "How did I get myself into this?" I asked. "Why is this happening to me? Why me?"

"Listen honey, unfortunately, young girls like you all over the country ask themselves that every single day. But I'm going to tell you what I would tell any of those girls. God has a plan for everybody, Asia," Ms. Coleman smiled. Although her smile was like a healing ointment to the pain I was feeling inside, I couldn't fix my own lips to display such optimism. "Now you just have to figure out what your plan is," she continued. "I know that you feel lost right now, but I am here for you; in any way that you need me to be." Ms. Coleman stood up straight, took a deep breath and then asked, "Does your aunt know yet?"

I shook my head and felt my tears return. "No ma'am. And there is no 'yet'. My aunt is the last person in the world I want to find out. If she finds out, she's going to kill me." I was not hypothetically speaking. My aunt was going to kill me if she found out I was carrying a child. I was not playing. She was literally going to choke the life out of me.

My aunt Joy had made it clear from the first day I had come to live with her that she was not into raising no babies that she didn't birth herself. That if I even thought about coming around with a baby, both me and the baby would be out on the streets. I remember on the first day of this school year when I got all dressed to impress with my Baby Phat skirt outfit and form fitting, signature Baby Phat tee with cap sleeves. She snatched me right up by the arm before I sauntered out the door knowing that I was the ish. "Yeah, you might be cute, but you ain't grown. So remember, if you even think about doing grown-up things, then you'll have to suffer the grown-up consequences. You are going to school to get with the books, not boys. So keep your legs closed and your mind open and we won't have any problems. Now have a good first day of school," she said before loosening my arm and lightly shoving me out the door.

I knew she wasn't joking either. She wasn't even completely sold on the idea of playing mommy to her brother's child, let along playing the role of grandmother at forty. Here I had done everything she told me not to. I knew beyond a doubt that she wouldn't be the kind, loving and understanding custodial guardian like all of those actresses cast in those *Lifetime* movies. She barely wanted to be bothered with me, so I knew that she would have a heart attack once she found out I was pregnant.

I had been living with my aunt for about a year now. She was my father's sister and had agreed to take me in after my father was murdered. He was shot to death when a couple of thugs tried to rob one of his pizza chain stores. It was crazy because he'd just recovered from gunshot wounds from an attempted home robbery. He'd only been out of the hospital and back to work a few weeks before he was gun downed in the pizza shop. My aunt was his only surviving family besides my half brother and me. My half brother isn't that much older than me, and he still lives with his mother. There was no way his mother was going to let me live with them, considering my mom stole my father from her. She hated on me like I was the one who hooked them up or something. Heck, I hadn't even been born when they hooked up. And the fact that my mother died while giving birth to me didn't make her accept me as her son's sister any better. But I could understand why she was tripping. Thankfully, though, my aunt Joy was there to keep me from having to go to some foster home or something.

Although I did not doubt that my aunt loved me, I did suspect that she did not appreciate me intruding in her everyday life. I had been a niece that she'd only seen on major holidays. After my daddy died, I became a permanent everyday fixture in her life. Now that I, too, was in a predicament to have a permanent fixture in my life, I could only imagine what she would do once she found out. Knowing my aunt Joy, she would do exactly what she said she'd do.

"I can't tell her," I enforced to Ms. Coleman.

"And I don't want you to tell her either." I shook my head and, once again, shuddered at the thought of my aunt finding out. "I don't want to tell her. I don't know what she is going to say, or even worse, what she is going to do," I admitted. "But I do know that she is going to hate me. She's going to put me out and then I'll have nowhere to go. I'll be living on the streets somewhere. And you know me Ms.Coleman, I am not one to be able to live on nobody's streets."

I shook my head, for a minute falling back into my prideful ways. Everyone knew me as the baddest and the hottest chick at Cass. What would I look like turning up homeless? I was getting all caught up in what other people would think of me. Just as soon as I felt the queasiness in my stomach, I was once again knocked down a peg or two, reminded of the terrible fix I was in.

"I highly doubt that, Asia," Ms. Coleman replied. "She is your family. She loves you, and because she loves you I'm sure she only wants the best for you and has plans of you graduating high school and going on to college. So, yes, she will probably be disappointed, but no matter what you do, she can never hate you, or put you out on the streets like a dog. Yeah, finishing high school and going on to college while raising a baby is going to be challenging, but it can be done. But no matter how grown and independent you think you might be, you are still going to need the help of the people who care about you. And I know your aunt cares about you, Asia."

I was listening to every word Ms. Coleman was saying, but I was not trying to hear it. She could tell she wasn't getting through to me by the way I rolled my eyes upward and turned my head. No disrespect was meant, but I refused to tell my aunt no matter how much she made it sound as though it was the right thing to do.

Ms. Coleman let out a sigh of defeat. "Look, Asia, I will even help you tell her if you'd like me to."

I could see that Ms. Coleman wasn't going to let up. I respected her enough to know that she wouldn't give me wrong advice. So I thought for a minute as I wiped the remnant of tears from my face while reconsidering everything she'd said. "I don't know. I just don't think that I can," I told her.

"You have to, Asia. This isn't something that you can keep from your aunt. She has to know. Besides, it will get to a point where you have to tell her. I mean, eventually you are going to start showing.

What are you going to do when your belly begins to grow? She will know that you are pregnant and will be even more upset that you did not come to her. Plus, you need medical attention to make sure that your baby is healthy. Prenatal care is very important for both the well being of yourself and your baby. No matter what decision you make regarding your pregnancy, you are going to have to eventually tell your aunt anyway. More than likely, since you are underage, you will need her to sign some type of paperwork. Trust me when I tell you this, Asia, you are not ready to handle this by yourself," Ms. Coleman stated firmly. "So why don't I set up an appointment with your aunt so that together we can tell her what's going on with you?"

"No!" I exclaimed. The more Ms. Coleman talked about the baby, the more real it became and the more scared I got. I couldn't take care of myself, let alone a baby. I couldn't do this. I couldn't. "I . . . I . . . I don't have to tell her if I get an abortion. I don't want this baby. I don't need a baby right now. I'm sure there is a way that I can get rid of it without her ever knowing anything about it," I stated.

"Asia," Ms. Coleman said with a sigh.

The sad tone in her voice made me look up at

her. The tears that had accumulated in her eyes surprised me. I mean, why was she crying? She wasn't the one who was underage, desperate, and pregnant.

"I can't tell you what to do, and I'm not here to pass judgment on you," she said to me with such sincerity, "but I will not let you make this decision on your own. You need to speak with your aunt about this. I can't allow you to make a choice that you might regret in the future. You are young and afraid. I understand that, but this is something that you have to consult your family about. An abortion is a huge decision. There are millions of women who would love to have children but cannot. The life that you are carrying inside of your stomach is precious. You have a responsibility to make the best choice along with your aunt. Even though it is unexpected and untimely, it is a blessing from God."

Right about now I was fed up hearing about God, His plans and His blessings. I've heard folks say that God is good, all the time. Well, this time I couldn't find one thing good when it came to the situation I was in. If God had anything to do with it, if this was part of His plan, and if He thought for a minute me getting knocked up would be a blessing, then I could do without all that God business for sure. I didn't want God's plan, God's blessing, or this baby, and Ms. Coleman needed to know that no matter what she said.

"I don't want a baby right now," I cried, throwing myself a pity party even though I knew that I only had myself to blame for my current predicament.

"But you have one and now you have to think of not only what's best for you, but for everyone involved. You took it upon yourself to have unprotected sex, so now you have to go about this situation in the right way, and that includes telling your aunt," Ms. Coleman preached.

"I'm only seventeen," I whispered. "I'm just a baby myself."

"And now it is time for you to grow up." Ms. Coleman now had sternness about her tone. She walked over to her desk and opened one of her desk drawers. She grabbed her car keys and her purse. She then walked over to the door, unlocked it and said, "Let's go."

"Go? Where are we going?" I asked in confusion. "I still have classes to attend."

"I think this is a little bit more important. I will

write you a pass to give to your teachers. We are going to speak with your aunt." Ms. Coleman looked down at her watch. "She's works third shift right? Will she be home now or did she pick up an extra shift?

I froze and the trepidation that filled my heart caused my breathing to speed up. "What? Right now? But I said that I didn't . . ."

"This is not something that you should procrastinate on," she said, cutting me off. "I'm here for you, Asia. Don't you trust me?"

I remained silent. Ms. Coleman looked at me with pleading eyes. Of course I trusted her, but I was just a scared, unwed, pregnant, high school teenager.

"You wouldn't have told me what was going on with you if you didn't trust me, Asia," she said. "I promise, I will help you through this. Let's go deal with your aunt together," she said as she reached for my hand.

I stood from my seat and took her hand as I wiped my face dry. We walked out of the school hand in hand. I managed to keep dry eyes all the way until we made it out to the school parking lot. By then, my tears were like an unstoppable faucet.

Ms. Coleman squeezed my hand reassuringly the entire way to the car. As I got into her car, I thought back to how I had gotten myself into this mess in the first place. My mind wandered back to when it all began. It all started on the first day of school.

Chapter One

I couldn't believe I was back again for another year at Cass High School. Everyone in Detroit knew that Cass was the best and most popping school in the entire city. I remember when I first entered high school my dad and my stepmother wouldn't allow me to attend Cass. They'd sent me to a private school instead. In my sophomore year I had been able to convince them that they could save a lot of money by allowing me to attend Cass. Of course my greedy stepmother was happy to oblige. All that meant was more money left for her to spend. I wasn't a few months into the school year when they separated. I'd seen that she was a gold digger from the jump, but it had taken my dad a minute. Better sooner than later though.

And who cared as long as I had gotten what I wanted out of the deal, which was to spend my remaining high school years at the livest school in the Midwest.

The first day there I couldn't believe that I was finally stepping foot inside of it. I had wanted to go to Cass ever since I was in the sixth grade. See, all of my older cousins had passed through the hallways at Cass and they represented the school to the fullest even after they had graduated and moved on to college. Everybody knew that it was the school where the popular kids went. All of the girls were considered Dime Pieces and all of the boys were too cool for school, some were even highly recognized athletes.

I remember it just like it was yesterday. I couldn't believe that I had finally arrived, and as I stepped off of the school bus, I looked up at my new school. Fresh into sixteen, I was geeked for my first day of school. That same feeling still existed now that I was seventeen.

The past couple of months of my life had been rough. I had lost my father and had been sent to live with my aunt. I guess it was safe to say that my life had changed in a drastic way. My daddy had owned pizza parlors all over the city, so we were very well off and I never wanted for anything when he was alive. I missed him and the lifestyle that he had provided for me. My aunt Joy was nice and I loved her, but she struggled as a nurse and could barely make enough money to take care of herself, let alone me. Needless to say, I was forced to adjust to a more meager way of living.

At first, when my aunt took me in, I think she thought that a bag of money came attached to me. My dad's estate attorney nipped her dreams in the bud when he informed her of how much money my father owed in back taxes as a result of his businesses having suffered when the economy took a turn for the worse. Since he'd only been separated from his wife and the divorce had not been finalized, she had control of any life insurance policies. The IRS pretty much owned everything we thought was my father's, right down to the casket they buried him in. I wish I'd known how bad off things really were for my father, but being his little girl, he never let on about his money problems. He continued to give me all that my heart desired until the day he died.

I missed my daddy terribly and there were some days when I would do nothing but cry. For some reason, going back to school to hang out with some of my old friends felt uplifting. It had been a long time since I had felt up about anything. For some reason, I was convinced that this high school year was going to be ten times better than any other level of schooling that I had surpassed. I hoped the new experiences would help me forget all of my troubles.

I didn't have it going on like I did in the past. I still had a lot of my expensive material things, but heck, anybody who stayed on the latest fashion trends knew that stuff was out dated. My souped-up car that had been a sweet sixteen birthday present from my father well, that belonged to the IRS too. But in spite of the fact that I was in reverse upgrade mode, I was still determined to become 'That Girl' the same way I had been when I started Cass High.

Out of all the girls in my class, I had most wanted to be 'Miss It'. The same went now that I was entering my junior year. Heck, even back as a freshman in the private school I was already a few steps ahead of the game, because even though I was young, I was built like some of the upper class girls. I was what guys would call thick. I had wide hips, a big ol' ghetto girl booty, and a slim waist. Through it all, I'd managed to maintain that eye catching physique.

On top of my build, I looked completely different than most of the light skinned, bright eyed, chicks walking around Cass High School. I was dark. I mean dark, dark; like the sun had birthed me itself. My hair was long and thick while my eyes were as bright as my perfect smile. I rocked the hottest gear thanks to my new best friend, Tracey.

Tracey and I had been friends for about five years now, but it wasn't until recently that I went ahead and gave her the title of 'best friend.' Tracey was younger than me. She was only fourteen going on fifteen. I usually didn't run with underclassmen, but my original Cass crew had pretty much been dismantled by life's circumstances. Tracey was cool people though, and on top of that, she was a hustler. Besides being a full-time student in school, Tracey boosted clothes on the side.

I already know what folks are thinking; what is she doing boosting clothes at 14? But see, Tracey was not the typical fourteen year old girl. She had been around the block and back a couple of times due to growing up in a household full of older brothers. Her brothers all hustled and they all lived with their grandmother who could not keep up with any of them even if she wasn't almost eighty years old, suffering from diabetes and death in her right ear. Like most youth in that type of situation, Tracey and her brothers turned to the streets for guidance.

When I wanted freedom, not that my aunt was overly strict on me and all up in my business to begin with, but it was to Tracey's house I would go to. It just gave me that grown up feeling. At Tracey's, we could do what we wanted, when we wanted, how we wanted and didn't have a care in the world. There was no one there to hold us accountable for our actions. With Tracey living the way she was living and my aunt working third shift as a nurse, plus being on call at all hours, I knew that Tracey and I together would run Cass this year before the first semester was over. We were young, fly, and flashy as we walked into the high school together arm in arm.

"Girl, I cannot believe that I am finally here!" Tracey said excitedly. "The infamous Cass High School." She pulled her schedule out of her book bag. "And can you believe we even have a class together?"

"I know. That ninth grade algebra has got me stuck. But I'm going to get through it with a passing grade this year if it kills me," I said as we maneuvered our way through the sea of people that cluttered the halls, some standing around catching up with peeps they hadn't seen all summer, and others trying to locate their home rooms.

"And I'm going to help you pass it," Tracey replied. "That way maybe we can even be in geometry together too."

I finally helped Tracey locate her homeroom. "I'll hook up with you at lunch." I pulled my schedule out. "You do have it sixth period, right?" Tracey double checked her schedule before confirming that she did have lunch the same period as me. "Then I'll see you later." I then headed to my own homeroom where I bumped into a girl named Rena who I recognized from last year. We entered the class while laughing with one another.

"Ladies, quiet down please and have a seat."

We both stopped and turned to look at the older black man sitting behind the teacher's desk in the front of the class.

"Uh-oh, it looks like he is going to be a lot of fun," I whispered to Rena as I rolled my eyes and walked down the aisle to find a seat at the back of the class.

Everybody knew that only brown nosers and the smart kids sat up front, and even though I was no dummy, I knew it was better not to be labeled as one of the A-students in school. It was like social suicide, so I was determined to not be the star student of my class.

All of the students chatted quietly amongst themselves as we watched last minute stragglers wander into the room right before the tardy bell rang. The old man behind the desk did not take any initiative to get the class started, so we did not take the initiative to shut up and pay attention. Mumbled chatter went on throughout the room. Every individual clique had their own conversations, making the language in the room sound foreign.

Back in middle school the teacher would have never allowed so much nonsense to be going on, so the fact that high school was so much more lenient only made me love it that much more. I think the teachers at the high schools let the kids get away with more disruptive behavior in the classroom because most of the students were as big as, if not bigger, than the teachers. So they were probably scared to take authority over them. That and the fact that they were probably scared of their ghetto parents who might try to come up to the school and get with them if they dared to discipline their child. The old adage of "It takes a village" had been put to rest by the new generation of parenting.

It wasn't until a caramel colored woman in a nice red skirt suit walked into the room that all of the chatter ceased. She looked as if she could have been someone's older sister. She looked much too young to be a teacher, yet the school badge that she wore identified her as a staff member.

"Hello students, can I please have your attention?" she stated loudly enough for us to hear her, but quietly enough to keep her ladylike status intact.

We all looked up and stopped speaking as the woman stood confidently in front of us. "My name is Ms. Coleman and I am the new high school guidance counselor here at Cass. Every year the guidance counselors like to take a minute to visit the home room classes and welcome the students into the school. I am here to extend that welcome."

I watched her demeanor. She was pretty, very pretty, and her smile was polite and sincere. She had my full attention as she continued.

"I'd like to welcome back those returning Cass students as well as those who are new to the school. Since I'm new myself, I don't recognize any of you, but I'd love to get to know you all. So feel free to stop by my office any time just to introduce yourselves to me, have lunch with me, talk, etc . . ."

Her invitation seemed genuine, and by the looks on some of the faces around me, some would just take Ms. Coleman up on her offer.

"I know that dealing with high school and all that comes along with it can sometimes be overwhelming. There are a lot of things that can distract you from your education. Some of these things are peer pressure, drugs, sex . . ."

Everybody in the class giggled at the mention of sex and made side jokes about it before she raised her hand to grab our attention again. "Okay guys, listen up." After we all quieted down again she finished. "I want you all to know that my door is always open to you. If you ever need to talk about *anything*, know that I've been there done that and can probably give you some good advice."

"You look like you're in high school yourself," a boy called out. "You ain't really some nark or something are you?" Once again, the class giggled.

Ms. Coleman went on to tell us her age and how she'd graduated from high school early, then went on to college to study education and psychology. We were convinced that no matter how young she was, she was definitely qualified to be in the position that she was in.

"Don't be afraid to come to me if you have a

problem and even if you aren't having any problems," Ms. Coleman told us. "I would love for you to just drop into my office to say hi. I always have snacks and candy available too, so stop by to see me sometime. Again, welcome to your junior year at Cass High School. This is going to be a very exciting school year. I look forward to working with you guys and helping you out in the year ahead. Those of you who are new to Cass like myself, alright fresh meat," she joked with a flattering smile, "Pay attention to Mr. Reiner here," she pointed to the man behind the desk, "and cut out all that talking that was going on when I walked in." She gave us a wink. "Bye." She waved as she left the room.

"Bye!" most of us sang out in unison.

"She was cool," I turned and said to Rena who had taken a seat behind me. She had already put her head down on the top of her desk and had begun to drift off to sleep. I smirked and shook my head. It was only the first day of school and she was already slacking off. Mr. Reiner, my first hour teacher, finally stood and began his lesson. I opened my note book and paid attention. Hey, it was the first day of school. I figured I may as well play the role of good student . . . for now.

I survived through my first class, and so far, nothing seemed so different this year of school than any other year at any other school.

"You got your books for the next class?" I asked Tracey when I saw her in the hallway.

"Yeah, I think I have them in my book bag," she replied as she began comparing her schedule to the books she had in her bag.

"If you need to get your books out of your locker, I'll walk with you and then show you where your next class is," I stated.

"Cool, because I think I forgot one," she said.

We both strutted our stuff through the halls and I leaned against a row of lockers next to Tracey's as she arrived at her own and retrieved her books. That's when I saw him, Pierce Watson. He was looking fine in his leather varsity jacket and baggy street jeans accompanied by fresh sneakers; Jordan's to be exact. He was posted on the wall with a crowd of people around him, and to my surprise, he was staring my way.

I had never seen him before. I don't know if it was because he was new at Cass, or if I just hadn't paid him any attention in the past, so busy with my own clique. But I knew that he had to be older than me, much older. He had a very mature look about him. So, either he'd started school late, or he'd flunked classes and was a career high school student. Either way it went, I was digging his style. He was so comfortable amongst his friends, and the fact that he played a varsity sport was a dead giveaway.

I blushed slightly and then forced myself to turn around. I had almost forgotten that Tracey was even standing there. For a minute there I felt like I was in some corny high school movie where everything is in slow motion. All the other voices around fade out and it's like it's just the lead girl and guy standing there. I was hoping that Tracey hadn't witnessed the brief scene.

"You ready?" I asked Tracey after clearing my throat.

She nodded, as we started walking off, but when she noticed the look on my face she said, "What's up? Why are you all giddy and acting shy?" She smiled deviously as she looked around.

"Girl, I'm straight. Just happy to be back at Cass I suppose." I smacked my lips and changed the subject as I headed down the hall in the opposite direction of the fine upperclassmen.

"Humph, you could have fooled me." Tracey's tone was that of disbelief.

"Whatever. I am not acting giddy. I just don't want to be late for class."

"I thought you said that you were just happy to be back at . . ."

"Here we are," I said, cutting Tracey off, relieved that we were standing outside of her next class. "See you at lunch." I quickly took off before Tracey could say anything else. Hopefully by lunch she would have forgotten all about my peculiar behavior.

Unfortunately, I was the one who couldn't forget. Throughout the entire day I found myself thinking about the boy's face. He was so fine, and each time I tried to focus on what was going on in the classroom, I found my mind wandering back to him. I was sprung and didn't even know the boy's name. I made a mental note to correct that.

Besides developing a new crush on a boy that I didn't even know, the first day of school was basically uneventful. At lunch time Tracey and I just pretty much spent the entire period people watching and scoping out my prospective competition of being the head chick in charge. As far as I was concerned, there was none.

When the final bell rang, I met back up with Tracey on the ground floor at her locker. She gave me a brief recap of her first day at Cass. Her day had been equally uneventful, except for her getting lost and ending up in the wrong class. The teacher took attendance and then asked if there was anyone's name that she hadn't called. Tracey raised her hand. After the teacher double checked her roster and compared it to Tracey's schedule, they realized that Tracey had ended up in the wrong class.

After listening to Tracey tell me how embarrassed she was I assured her that it was no big deal. Afterwards I told her that I would catch her later. I then headed out to catch my bus. I was halfway there when I remembered I had left my purse and house keys in my locker. I checked my watch and saw that I only had about five minutes before my bus took off without me. I didn't have much time, so I took off running, heading to the third floor.

When I arrived at my locker I was out of breath and I hurriedly put in the combination. I snatched my purse from the metal hook and ran all the way outside just as the buses were pulling out of the parking lot. I jogged after it, yelling, "Wait!" but stopped when I realized it was too late. I had missed my bus and it was at least an hour walk to get to my house. Now I was the one who was embarrassed. I'd been known to drive a car that cost more than what the teacher's got paid annually, and now here I was labeled as a bus rider. And it's not like I could even hide the fact considering I looked like a fool chasing it while the kids on the buses pointed and laughed. This was not the road towards being "That Chick," but with my style and class, I'm sure I could recover easily. But for now, I felt like I was up the creek without a paddle.

Auntie was at work, so I knew that I was out of luck. And it wasn't like I carried around the $200 weekly allowance my dad used to give me, so I didn't have bus fair. And catching the city bus was absolutely out of the question. I'd rather be seen walking than waiting at the bus stop. So, I didn't have a choice, but to get my stroll on.

As I headed for home, my head hung low. I didn't even want to look up and see who might spot me. For some reason I was just as embarrassed to be walking as I was if I were taking public transportation. It was weird, but I just felt like everybody who was still around was watching me. The cheerleading team was outside practicing and the basketball players were lingering around outside waiting for their practice to begin. It was just my luck that Mr. Tall, Fine, and Popular was standing amongst the group that I had to walk past in order to exit school property. I was nervous as I made my way past them.

"Dang, I didn't know fresh meat came cooked like that," one of the players shouted as if I couldn't hear him, or maybe he just did not care if I heard him.

"Yeah shorty is fine," I heard another add.

"Freshman are coming in bigger, better and finer packages these days," I heard the first player who had spoken say.

"Nah, ol' girl ain't no freshman." The other one added his two cents again. "I remember seeing her last year. You probably just don't recognize her because you could hardly see her face with her nose all tooted up in the air." A few chuckles followed his comment.

I was so self conscious that I stumbled on the cracked concrete and my book bag fell open, spilling some of the contents onto the ground. I closed my eyes as I heard the laughter of the guys. I didn't see what was so funny of course. As simple as it may have been, I was mortified and embarrassed. I bent down to retrieve my belongings as tears burned my eyes. Out of nowhere the boy that I had noticed earlier kneeled down in front of me.

"You alright?" he asked with a smile as he helped me pick up my things. I could tell he wanted to join in on the laughter of his friends as he fought to keep the slight smirk from cracking through.

"Go ahead, you can laugh," I said angrily. "You don't have to help me. I can pick up my own stuff."

He chuckled a little bit. "You've got two left feet ma," he said with a friendly smile. "It figures somebody as pretty as you would have to have a flaw. You were cursed with clumsiness."

I smiled and shook my head. I was so embarrassed that if I were light skinned, my face would have been fire red.

"I'm not clumsy," I defended. "It was an accident." I snatched one of my folders from his hand and finally stood once I had gathered myself.

"An accident, huh?" He looked me up and down. "Either that or you just ain't used to walking."

He had the latter part correct. I wasn't used to walking, not like this. Walking the school halls looking fly? Yeah. Walking through the mall grabbing up anything my heart desired? Yeah, that too. But walking to get from A to B? Now that was another story for somebody to write.

"What's your name?" he asked me.

I was surprised as I looked up at his six foot frame. At 5'5" it felt like I was staring at a giant. "Asia," I replied shyly. I didn't know whether to be flattered that he wanted to know my name, or pissed that he didn't already know who I was. Even his boy with the fly mouth had recognized me from last year. I guess clothes and car don't make a man, but they sure do make a girl . . . obviously to the point where she's unrecognizable without all the bling and material things. Heck, I almost felt as though I had to make a whole new fresh start.

"I'm Pierce," he introduced. When he put his arm around my shoulder I thought I was going to die. That's when I heard the cheerleaders take notice.

"Ooh Miranda, it looks like somebody is digging on your man, girl!" I heard one girl shout out.

"Where are we walking to Ms. Asia?" he asked, ignoring the comment the girl had just made. I knew if I had heard it, he had heard it too, but he didn't seem phased by it. So obviously, whoever Miranda was, she wasn't taking care of her business with her man, if in fact he was her man. At the rate I was going, he was about to be somebody's man; mine.

I turned around to look at the group of mostly hating upper class senior girls who had stopped their practice to be all up in my business.

"I'm walking home, but you might want to go back to what you were doing. Miranda might get mad," I teased as I focused my attention back on him.

He laughed. "Miranda ain't my girlfriend. I'm good right here," he replied. "I saw you checking out the kid earlier today. Next time come holla at me."

"What? Boy, wasn't nobody checking you out. If anything, you were feeling me," I said as I got more comfortable in his presence. I had to counter him and hide the fact that I had been checking on him earlier by Tracey's locker.

"True dat," he replied quickly.

His response surprised me. As cool and as slick as he came across, he didn't even try to hide the fact that he had been scoping me out. I liked that in a man; honesty. I looked forward as we continued to walk.

"How far away do you live from here?" he asked.

"My house is about an hour away on foot. You don't have to walk me there. I know you have practice. Thanks for helping me with my stuff, though, but I don't want to put you out," I said as I stopped and turned to face him. If I was Pinocchio, my nose would have grown. Lord knows that I wanted that boy to walk me home. And I didn't want him to stop there. I wanted him to walk me down the aisle while he was at it.

"I've got a whip. You want me to give you a ride to your crib?" he asked as he pulled out his car keys. "I can take you real quick and be back in time for practice. I won't miss much." He looked over his shoulder back at his boys. "Plus, I'm the star player. If this team was pro I'd be the franchise." He popped the collar on his jacket.

He was cocky to say the least, but I liked that about him. Only a girl like me could appreciate that type of confidence in a man.

"Thanks, but no thanks. My aunt will trip if I roll up to her house with a boy after the speech she gave me this morning," I answered truthfully.

"Oh yeah, you're a youngin' huh? How old are you anyway? About fifteen?"

"Young, but old enough," I said in a flirtatious tone. "But if you want me to be fifteen, then fifteen it is."

He looked at me skeptically and then turned me around and replied, "I don't know, you just might be, but you got a whole lot going on to be just fifteen." I knew he was peeping my backside.

"Are you always that blunt?" I asked.

"Do you always lie about your age?" he shot back.

I rolled my eyes and put my hands on my hip. "I didn't lie," I shot back. "I said I'd be whatever age you wanted me to be. Heck, your boy thought I was only a freshman. So if you like 'em young, and that's what I have to be in order to be down, then in that case, I'm only fourteen." I winked. I needed Pierce to know that he had met his match in me. He may have thought he was "That Dude," but I knew for a fact that I was "That Chick." "Especially if that helps you feel like you all grown and things," I added.

"Sixteen ain't grown," he replied. "So even if you were only fourteen, I'd still have two more years to make you my girl before it's against the law. So quit playing, girl, how old are you?"

I smiled and started walking backwards towards my house as I gave him the once over. I couldn't believe he was only sixteen trying to get his grown man on. Out in the streets, I could have easily mistaken him to be about nineteen years old. "I better get going. I have a ways to walk so I'll talk to you later." I gave him one last flirtatious look, wondering how he'd managed to become top dog of the Cass basketball team. I made a mental note to myself that this year I'd have to get into the school spirit and check out way more sporting events. Look what I had been missing.

"Yeah alright," he replied. "I'll holla at you later." He put up a peace sign and jogged back over to his friends while I turned to continue my journey home.

I couldn't believe that I had just held a conversation with this boy who had my mind tripping on him all day, and come to find out he's just a baby. I know him being a year younger than me isn't much in the real world, but in high school it's like dog years. Of course, had our ages been reversed it would have been different, because it was more cool for a younger girl to talk to an older guy.

Keeping in mind what the late, great songstress, Aaliyah, said about age being nothing but a number, I couldn't wait to get home to tell Tracey. She was on my must call list. I had to tell her about Mr. Pierce.

Now that I had formally met him, I was even more intrigued by him. I no longer cared that I had to walk home, because if I had made my bus, I would have never bumped into Pierce. I guess everything does happen for a reason. I quickly concluded that the three mile stroll was worth it.

I smiled as I thought of the gossip that would be

all over school by morning. My name would be on every girl's tongue by first period. I had heard the jealousy in the cheerleader's voices when they had seen Pierce and me together, so I knew that I had stepped on some girl's toes. From the sounds of it, the girl's name was Miranda.

Chapter Two

"You talked to who?" Tracey shouted into the phone.

"Pierce," I responded as if it was no big deal.

"You lie!" she accused. I could practically hear her smile through the phone she was so excited. "I promise, in almost all of my classes someone mentioned his name. Word is, he be ballin' like crazy for the Cass Varsity B-Ball team and is probably going to go pro one day. You do know he's not a senior right? Chicks know he's going to be banking someday, so they trying to be his high school sweetheart now so that they don't look like gold diggers trying to get at him once he makes the big league . . ." Tracey went on and on and on. "What did he say to you? Did he mention me?" she asked.

I had to stop her right there. "Mention you? Why would he mention you?"

"You know that I think he is cute. I told you I was trying to date the most popular boy in school this year and he is it," Tracey said. "Can you imagine if I, a freshman chick, dated Pierce. Ooooh the sistas would be hatin'!"

I frowned. I knew exactly what Tracey was trying to do. She was trying to stake her claim to Pierce before I got a chance to do it so that he would be off limits to me. Everybody knows that you can't date any boy that your best friend is interested in; it did not matter if the guy did not even know the girl existed. If Tracey liked Pierce, then I could not, and because she had voiced her interest in him first, he was technically hers.

"Since when do you like him? You have never mentioned anything about him before," I stated, trying to hide the fact that I was mad and a little salty that she had called dibs on a boy that I had talked to first. "And I know you saw that little eye contact he and I had by your locker this morning."

"Girl, what are you talking about. I didn't even notice Pierce. I must have been too busy at my locker, because had I noticed him, I would have gone over and spoke to him."

"Oh, so you're bold like that all of a sudden?" I asked. "You can just spot a cute guy you think you might like and go walk up to him and spit game out of the blue?"

"What do you mean out of the blue? I've always liked him. Even when we were in middle school, but he was too old for me back then. Now I'm in high school and he is just my type. I think I'm going to get at him tomorrow," she said confidently, oblivious to the fact that I was steaming on the inside.

"Whatever," I said. I rolled my eyes to the ceiling. The conversation with Tracey was old and I was about ready to hang up on her lying butt. Not once could I ever recall her mentioning having a crush on some dude named Pierce. And I know darn well she saw him and me eyeballing each other this morning. I'd known Tracey for a grip and she'd always been cool people. I hope high school wasn't about to change her into a backstabber. Many good friendships had become a casualty of high school self-centered drama. I hope Tracey's and mine wouldn't be one of them.

"Hold on girl, I think I hear my auntie calling me." I pulled the phone away from my ear. I knew Auntie Joy was not due home any time soon, but still I yelled, "Huh? Okay ma! Here I come. Just give me one second!" I got back on the phone and said, "Tracey, girl, I've got to call you back. My aunt needs me to help her with something."

"Okay girl, I will . . ."

Click!

I hung up before she could finish her sentence. I threw the cordless phone on my bed and logged onto my computer to check out Facebook on the mini laptop notebook, one of the last gifts my father had gotten me before he died.

After a while I hopped up to start my chores before my aunt really did get home. I wasn't trying to hear her mouth if I did not do them. She was always hollering about responsibility and taking initiative now that I was older, so to avoid another lecture, I began to wash the dishes. It didn't take me very long. I turned on my Chris Brown CD, putting the volume on blast, and by the time the entire disc had played, I was done. Not five minutes later my aunt walked through the door, wearing colorful hospital scrubs and looking exhausted.

"Asia, why must you blare that radio like that? Turn that down!" she fussed. It never failed; she always had something to say. I think my aunt was the only person in the world who could always find something to fuss about. If she died and went to heaven, she'd probably find something to complain about. Heck, if she died and went to hell, she'd probably even get on the devil's nerves.

"Hey Auntie Joy," I said as I gave her a kiss on the cheek. "How was work?" You'd think I'd learn to stop asking that question by now, but for some reason, out of habit I did it every day she came in from work.

"Don't worry about my job. As long as I have one and is taking care of your little spoiled booty, that's all you need to know. I don't want you having to worry about grown-up things. Enjoy being a kid while it lasts," she stated as she flopped down on our worn sofa. "Because pretty soon, you gon' be working just as hard as me to make ends meet." She flopped down on the couch and exhaled as she removed her shoes. "How was school?"

"It was okay," I said as I was instantly reminded of Tracey stealing my wannabe crush

"Just okay?" she asked. "I hear you and your little girlfriend talk about that school like it's Harvard Law School or something, and it was just okay? Come on, you got to come better than that. It was your first day back at high school, new friends, new teachers. . . . Humor me with the details. I need some humor after the long day I had."

"Well . . ." I started as I got all starry eyed and sat down in the chair across from her. "The most popular boy in school talked to me today," I admitted with a smile.

"A boy?" my aunt repeated as if she had heard me wrong. Her eyes scanned me up and down. "Did you not hear a word I said this morning?"

"Ugghh," I said as I stood up, forgetting that I was talking to the wrong person about how my day had really gone.

My aunt looked me up and down. "And did you wear that little skirt to school? I bet if you bend over I can see your pubic hairs. No wonder the most popular boy in the school talked to you. He trying to make you the most popular girl, and not in a good way. Heck, wearing that short little skirt, I'm surprised every boy in the school didn't talk to you." She said under her breath, "and ya'll wonder why the teacher's can't keep their hands off the students these days. Ol' hot tail girls."

I sighed, wishing that this conversation had never taken place.

"Answer me," my aunt spat. "Did you wear that to school?"

I wasn't trying to be disrespectful by not answering her. It's just that she had been talking so much that I really didn't think she had wanted me to answer. I nodded and looked down at my outfit. "Yeah, I wore this. Why? It's not a too sho . . ." Before I could even get a chance to tell her that it wasn't too short, she cut me off and started going on and on again.

"Like I said, no wonder he talked to you today." She looked at my outfit again. "I can't believe I didn't catch that this morning. I've told you about wearing those short little skirts and skin tight pants." She shook her head. "I can't believe my brother used to let you dress like that, bless his soul. Your clothes send the wrong message to these horny, hard headed little hoodlums. That boy probably talked to you because you put yourself out there for him like steak on a platter. Don't think you are about to get up to that high school and get fast. I don't want no hot in the tail teenage daughter. You are not grown, so don't be coming up in here talking about no boys. You need to be focused on your books, because I can barely take care of you let alone a baby. I'm only forty and I'm too young to be a great auntie," she preached.

"Baby? Who said anything about that? See Auntie, that's why I don't talk to you now, because ain't nobody even say anything about having sex. I just said that I talked to a boy. I doubt I will bring you a grandbaby by just talking. I've never known anybody getting pregnant by having a conversation," I stated smartly. She got on my nerves. She thought that I was so stupid and I hated when she treated me like a child. I was old enough to take care of myself and I definitely was not thinking about having no babies.

"I know you aren't getting smart with me. You heard what I said, little girl. Stop trying to grow up so fast," she warned.

"Yes, ma'am," I answered in a deflated tone, knowing that there was no way I could possibly go up against my aunt Joy and win.

"Go do your homework while I fix dinner, it will be ready in a couple hours," she said, her monotone voice revealing her fatigue.

I nodded and walked to my room. I looked back at my aunt who leaned back on the couch and closed her eyes, while she rubbed her temples. Bright skinned, with jet black hair, and petite features, she was a beautiful woman, but she looked ten years older than what she actually was. One would think she had raised a brood of children as worn out as she appeared. Looking at her, I kind of understood why she hadn't welcomed the idea of taking me in with open arms. She seemed to work so hard, but yet had so little. The last thing I would ever dream of doing is to add to that.

Forget about adding another burden onto my auntie, what made her think I would want to add that kind of burden to myself? I didn't know why she thought I was trying to bring a baby home. I was not her. I didn't want to be living in the ghetto and stressing out over a dead end job. I had seen enough struggle watching her do it the short time I had lived with her, and the bad part about it was that she didn't do a very good job, because her own daughter ended up strung out.

That's right, my aunt knows a little something about being a mother. Her daughter ended up dying from a drug overdose before she turned eighteen. That was not something that I wanted for myself. I knew that my aunt didn't want that for me either, which was probably why she stayed on top of me the way she did. I understood the fact that she only wanted what was best for me, but sometimes she rode me way too hard. This just made me want to do things my own way even more.

I can't even lie. I knew that Auntie Joy loved me. She was a really good aunt and I loved her for taking me in while I had nowhere else to turn. Although she only came around enough times for me to count on one hand while I was coming up, she was there for me when I needed her to be. If it wasn't for her, I would have been a ward of the state after my father was killed. Fortunately she stepped up to the plate without thinking twice. Okay, maybe she thought more than twice, but at the end of the day, she took me in, and that's all that matters.

I appreciated how even though my aunt didn't have the kind of money my daddy had, when it came time to go shopping for school clothes, she tried her hardest to keep me up to date with the latest fashions. Sometimes she worked 18 hour shifts as a nurse in the emergency room just to be able to do it. I think she tried to compensate the fact that I had lost my father by buying me things. I figured as much because my dad tried to do the very same thing when it came to me not having a mother. Even though it doesn't make the pain go away, I appreciated her for trying.

Auntie Joy was working really hard to try to finish off what my father started by raising me, and although sometime she was a pain in the butt, I loved her for taking care of me. I knew some girls my age who had mothers who were addicted to drugs, or whose mothers stayed out all times of the night doing who knows what with who knows who. Fortunately, I did not have to deal with that type of extreme lifestyle. When my auntie took me in, I knew in a sense that she was giving up her life so that she could make sure mine was up to par. I was lucky. Not a lot of young girls had women to look up to like I did, so I guess I could not complain too much.

Once I got to my bedroom I lay across my bed and opened up my history book to study. I didn't get very far before my mind drifted from what was in front of me to words that had been spoken to me earlier that afternoon . . ." *I still got two years to make you my girl.*"

Chapter Three

Remembering Pierce's words made me smile to myself. But remembering Tracey's words also wiped the smile right off my face. *Too bad I can't talk to him,* I thought. I didn't know this boy from Adam, so perhaps I should just cut my losses now and erase him from my memory bank, giving Tracey full reigns to go after him since she called dibs on him. Yeah, it was true that she'd called dibs after he had already showed an interest in me, but that's what I get for trying to play cool and not just express how I felt when I first saw him in the hall.

I refocused, finished studying, and spent the rest of the night with my aunt. We ate a late dinner together just like we did every night. I couldn't boil a hot dog, so I always had to wait for my aunt to get home and prepare dinner. I made a mental note to sign up for home economics next semester so that I could surprise my aunt one day and have dinner prepared for her when she came home.

Auntie Joy was big on spending quality time. I'm not one hundred percent, but I think it was just her way of keeping an eye on me. So even though she worked most of the time, she made sure that we sat down like a family at dinnertime. Had we been a little closer, I supposed that would have been the time for me to share with her what was going on in my teenage life. But with the way Auntie Joy reacted to everything, I wasn't about to put myself out there like that.

When I first came to live here, I used to feel like I could talk to her about anything during our family time. I didn't hesitate to let her know how much it hurt to no longer have a mother or a father. But over time, it seemed like the more the grief wore off and I was able to start being myself again, the less compassionate my aunt seemed. At first I appeared to be this shy, quiet teenager, but then once the real me shined through, the real Auntie Joy was right there like a dark cloud waiting to rain on my parade before I could even think about pulling out an umbrella.

Ever since I started back hanging out with Tracey and just being a regular old teenager, my aunt has been riding me tough. It seems like every other sentence out of her mouth was about boys and staying on track or avoiding the possible pitfalls that my high school years could bring. This night at dinner was no different. I quickly tuned her out.

I don't know why grown-ups haven't realized that the more they tell us not to do something, the more we want to do it. Take Adam and Eve for example; the more God told Eve not to eat the fruit from that tree, the more she wanted to just take a bite. And then when she took a bite and realized how good it was at the time, she even talked Adam into partaking in the forbidden fruit with her. Well, Adam and Eve were grown and rebelled against God himself. So what in the world makes grown-ups think that us kids won't do the same when it comes to them? That's just how it is. We want to taste life for ourselves.

Teenagers don't even really need a good reason to rebel. Most of the time, we do adult things because we think we are ready to handle them. Actually we aren't, but preaching to us about it won't stop us from making mistakes. If anything, when my aunt told me not to have sex, it made me wonder what the big deal was about it. I hadn't even thought about sex until she brought it to my attention. My main focus had been on flossin' the latest fashions and just being the "It Chick" of Cass High School. But the more she spoke about it, the more I became curious about it. So she was the cause of my increasing interest, and did not even know it.

I finished eating then excused myself to my room to retire for the night. Of course, I could hardly sleep with thoughts of Pierce on mind.

The next day I made sure that I was extra cute going to school. I wore jean low rise Capri pants, a House of Dereon hoody and brown Hollister flip flops. My toes were cute with the French manicure tips. My hair was pulled up in a high ponytail with Chinese bangs. My Sephora lip gloss was popping. I was as confident as ever when I stepped off of my bus and headed towards the building. I met up with Tracey at the entrance.

"Hey chick, you look cute," she greeted.

"Thanks girl," I replied. I had completely forgotten that I had been light-weight mad at her the night before. We were like that. We had an on again off again friendship. We had beefed out with each other so many times I had lost count, but we were always down for each other no matter what.

We could get into it with one another, but if somebody else had a problem with either of us, we were ready to slick up our faces with Vaseline and pull out our razors to protect one another.

Being an only child in the home full-time, because my half-brother only came around on weekends if he did that, I did not have anybody to run to if I needed help or if I ran into neighborhood problems. Tracey and I had met when I was in sixth grade, and even though we'd gone months before and kicked it with our individual cliques, now, all these years later, we were still tighter than Prince's leather pants.

My fights were her fights and vice versa. My ace boon was an understatement when mentioning Tracey, which is why I had so easily forgotten her moving in on Pierce even though I knew she knew I had gotten to him first. We walked into the building together and we had at least fifteen minutes before our first class began. Breakfast was being served, and even though we had no intentions on eating, we headed towards the cafeteria anyway just to check out the scene.

We walked into the cafeteria and it seemed like all heads turned our way as soon as we stepped through the door. It was like one of those scenes out of a movie. The record definitely scratched and suddenly all of my confidence flew out of the window. I don't know why, but for some reason I began doubting my choice of clothing for the day. What I once thought was a perfect outfit, now felt too small. I looked down at myself and began to tug at my clothes uncomfortably.

"What is everybody looking at?" I whispered as we found our way to a table off in the corner.

As we passed the cheerleaders table, I heard giggles that only stemmed from an inside joke. I ignored them and sat down at the table. Once I sat down, the girls giggled again, but this time I was let in on the joke when I heard someone say, "She used to think she was all that, but now she's like Cinderella after the clock strikes midnight. Her fancy coach must have turned into a pumpkin, because now she's catching the bus to school."

I could feel humiliation flushing over me as I forced to keep it from showing on my face.

"What was that all about?" Tracey asked as she frowned and looked over at the cheerleaders.

I shrugged. "I don't know. They're just hating. They saw me talking to Pierce yesterday and I guess the girl with the side ponytail likes him. I think they said her name was Miranda," I explained.

Tracey waved her hand in dismissal. "I don't know why they are hating on you. You're not even the one who likes Pierce, I am. She needs to be worried about me taking her man."

I rolled my eyes. All of this was just too much, and it was only the second day of school. "I don't think she's his girlfriend. At least he said she wasn't," I added.

"Even if she was, it wouldn't matter," she replied. "She can't compete with all this." Tracey ran her hands down her side.

The last I checked, Tracey hadn't been this confident or this worried about boys. I guess whatever it is they put in high school water, she'd already taken a sip and got drunk off of it.

Tracey and I sat conversing with each other for the next couple of minutes, and eventually the cheerleaders found something else to talk about as well. I had completely forgotten about the entire Pierce dilemma that was brewing between me, the cheerleaders and Tracey. That was until Pierce caught my attention as he entered the cafeteria with a couple of his boys strolling with him.

It was like as soon as he walked into the cafeteria, nobody else was in the room but me and him. He didn't notice me of course, but I peeped everything about him. Tiny butterflies danced in my stomach, and Tracey's words began to sound like that character from Charlie Brown.

WOMP WOMP WOMP

That was all I heard, because I was too busy daydreaming about my crush. The ringing of the warning bell snapped me out of my trance. I stood and grabbed my book bag.

"You ready?" I asked.

"Yeah I'm ready," Tracey replied then stood up. That's when she noticed Pierce as well.

She pulled a sucker from her Coach purse and put it in her mouth. She was not slick. She was trying her hardest to look cute because we had to walk past Pierce and his clique just to get to class.

It's crazy how something as small as walking past a boy can be the most exciting moment of a teenage girl's day. I was anxious to see what would happen. Pierce had obviously flirted with me the day before, but he could have just been being nice. Besides, he had talked to me after school when there were few people around. Now the entire school was congregated in the commons, so he might not even acknowledge me. I was so nervous that I held my breath as I followed Tracey out of the room. I kept my eyes towards the floor as if I did not see him standing to my left. He was posted on a wall with one foot propped up against it and his book bag slung over one shoulder.

Right as I passed him, I felt a soft touch brushing against my arm. I looked down and allowed my eyes to concentrate on the hand, then the wrist and up the arm of the person who was gripping my elbow. Low and behold, Pierce had reached out and grabbed my elbow to get my attention. I stopped walking and turned around to face him.

"What up, youngin'?" he greeted with a wink as he pulled me near him.

"Hey," I greeted with a smile, acknowledging his and my little inside joke about me playing around with my age yesterday.

As people began to rush by us, we were reminded that we needed to get a move on it if we were going to be on time for class. Pierce instantly cut to the chase. "I'm gon' have to get your number, ma. That way whenever I'm thinking about you, I can hit you up," he stated.

"I didn't know you were thinking about me," I replied as I shifted my weight to one leg and placed a manicured hand on my hip. Flirting with a boy, especially one that was younger than me, was new to me. I know he was only a year my junior, but still, as they say, girls mature more quickly than boys. Nonetheless, because I didn't have much experience spitting game to boys, my game wasn't down yet. I was at a disadvantage because I wasn't quite able to recognize when or if Pierce was running game on me.

"Yeah you knew I was thinking about you, cuz you were thinking about me too," he answered with the sexiest smile I had ever seen. He was so cool. He never did too much, but was always relaxed and extra confident. His friends, and of course my biggest critic, Miranda, were standing around watching our interaction closely.

"Mmm, hmmm!"

I turned when I heard Tracey clear her throat. I had forgotten all about my girl even being there. When I was reminded of her presence, I noticed her from the corner of my eye. For some stupid reason I began to feel guilty, like I was pushing up on her boyfriend even though Pierce had no clue that Tracey was even digging him.

"Oh!" I exclaimed as Tracey cut her eyes at me. "Pierce this is my girl Tracey, Tracey this is . . ."

"Pierce Watson," she finished my introduction for me. "I know exactly who you are. Remember, we went to the same middle school? Besides that, I came to all your games last year. You be doing your thing on the basketball court."

I could even tell Tracey was lying about that last part. That girl knows darn well she hadn't been to none of the Cass basketball games. But then again, she might have tagged along with one or two of her brothers.

Pierce frowned and looked at me before switching his gaze to Tracey. "Nah, I don't think I remember you. But it's nice to meet you anyway, ma." He looked her up and down. He had to be checking her out because Tracey's body was hot. She was naturally thick, and needless to say, she was pretty in the face. She wouldn't have been my friend if she was ugly.

"You've seen me play, huh?" he asked Tracey.

"Yeah, I've seen you," Tracey had the biggest smile imaginable on her face as she began to stroke her lollipop with her tongue. "I said that I would try out for cheerleading so I could be your personal number one fan," she flirted. Her game was so whack and she was literally making me sick to my stomach the way she was throwing herself shamelessly at him. I looked at the clock and saw that I only had a few minutes to make it all the way to the third floor for my first hour.

"Alright, Tracey," I said, interrupting her conversation with Pierce. "I'm about to break out. I've got to get to class."

"A'ight, girl," Tracey replied distractedly, still all up in Pierce's grill. "I need to get to class too. I hope I can remember where it is." That was Tracey's way of opening up the door for Pierce to offer to walk her to her class.

Okay, now I didn't feel so bad about not really having any game. Because standing here looking at Tracey, I'd rather have no game at all than to have even a little bit of hers. I mean, I was embarrassed for the girl. I had to walk away.

"Yo, where you going?" Pierce asked as he pushed past Tracey to get to me.

"What do you mean? I'm going to class," I said over my shoulder with an attitude. I don't know why I took out my frustrations on him. I was really frustrated with myself for allowing Tracey to steal him from underneath my nose. She was my best friend. She was supposed to know when I liked somebody, and even if she liked him too, she was supposed to sacrifice for the sake of our friendship. I knew I was a hypocrite because the same thing I wanted from her, I should've been giving to her. But yet and still even a blind man could see that he was trying to get at me and could care less about her.

Tracey was hot on Pierce's trail. She followed him as he walked beside me.

"Wait I want to take you somewhere," he said to me.

I stopped walking and faced him. "Take me where?"

He looked over at Tracey who was all up in our business. "Technically, I shouldn't even be saying anything in front of your girl," he looked at Tracey with disdain, "because you're not supposed to know about it because you're only a freshman." He then turned back to face me. "But I want to take you to our ditch party," he stated.

"Ditch party?" Tracey chimed in. "That sounds cool."

Both Pierce and I cut our eyes at her and then focused back on each other.

"I can't skip class, Pierce. It's only the second day of school. What is there to ditch? We haven't even begun work yet. I think I might have to take a rain check," I said with a smile.

"Excuse us for a minute, Pierce," Tracey said as she pulled me a couple feet away. "Are you crazy?" she scolded me in a deep whisper.

"What?" I asked with my face all screwed up.

"Come on, Asia," she pleaded. "You know I like this boy. Please let's just go to the ditch party with him."

"Well, since you like him so much, you can go. I'm not stopping you," I said nastily.

"He didn't invite me, Asia! He invited you." Tracey threw her hands on her hips. "Are you blind or something, girl? Can't you see that he really wants me there, but since I'm only a freshman he couldn't just come right out and invite me because freshman aren't even suppose to know. He knows you are my girl and that if he invited you, then I'd come with you. So technically he didn't tell a freshman." She began winking. "Get it?" She pulled on my arm and practically began begging. "Come on, please!" she said as she then clasped her hands together desperately. "I really want to chill with him."

I couldn't believe this mess. Evidently somebody was blind, either me or Tracey, because we were not watching the same scenario play out. That was for sure. "Fine, but you owe me," I shot back, giving in to Tracey's request.

"Thank you, thank you, thank you, best friend," she smiled as she and I walked back over to Pierce.

"I must really like you, ma. I don't wait for anyone," he said.

I knew the words were meant for me, but obviously Tracey thought she deserved them too.

"I guess you do like me then, because you waited," she replied with a smile. "But trust me, you'll find out soon enough that it was definitely worth the wait. Now where is this party?" Tracey then had the nerve to link her arm through his.

He looked at her like she was crazy. He then looked at me as if to say, "Is this girl serious?" But he just chuckled it off and didn't say anything off the chart as he started walking with Tracey in tow. I guess he bit his tongue to avoid hurting her feelings.

I followed behind the two of them trying my best not to laugh out loud.

"Where are we going?" I asked as I noticed us go down a flight of steps that I didn't even know existed.

"This part of the school was sealed off about ten years ago after they built the new addition. Nobody comes down here anymore," Pierce stated.

"It's dark. I can't see anything," I said.

The next thing I knew, Pierce turned loose from

Tracey and came and escorted me by the arm. "Be careful, ma," he called to me over his shoulder.

The way that he called me ma was so cool. His words melted me every time he said it, and my stupid self answered to it as if it was my birth name. I knew Tracey was steaming with jealousy. I could practically feel it coming off of her, but it served her right for pushing up on Pierce in the first place. There was already a little bit of tension between the two of us. I could tell that, from this point on, temperatures were only going to rise.

We walked into an area with a group of kids, and I instantly noticed that Tracey was the youngest one there. And of course, with her being my sidekick, it made me look all young minded too.

"What are they doing here, Pierce?" Miranda asked as she walked up to us, accompanied by her little cheerleading entourage of course. She looked at me like I was the ugliest thing on the face of the earth.

"They're chilling," he answered, "with me."

I guess that was enough of an answer, because she smacked her lips and turned on her heels with an attitude. Her girls followed her, but before they walked off we heard one of them say, "I didn't know we were running a freakin' day care." And of course they did their stupid giggling thing.

Tracey just sucked her teeth and rolled her eyes.

"Yo, Jake?" we heard Pierce say as he walked off. Not knowing what else to do, and not about to stand there and be everyone's target, we followed him.

Pierce walked over to his boys. "Tracey, this is my boy, Jake. Jake, this is Tracey. Show her a good time for me, fam," he stated as he politely handed Tracey over to Jake.

Tracey's jaw hit the floor when Pierce turned to me and put his arm around my shoulders then pulled me into him.

"Now that I got rid of your girl," he whispered in my ear, "you and me can chill."

"Who said I wanted to chill with you?" I asked, playing hard to get.

"Whatever, ma. You know the deal. Come and keep me company." He didn't have to ask me a third time. I fell right into the mix of being in his presence. We sat down and cuddled on a huge bean bag chair that was on the floor.

"You skip class like this all the time?" I asked him.

"Not all the time, just every Wednesday. We come down here to relax."

"And you mean to tell me that the teachers don't even know about this?" I said as I looked around.

"You didn't," was his reply.

I guess he told me.

Pierce started playing in my hair and the attention he was showing me made me feel special. I silently relished in the jealous looks that Miranda and her girls threw me. I obviously had what they wanted and that was Pierce's spotlight. He was 100% focused on me as we talked and laughed with each other. I was so carefree in discussing my life with him. At that moment he felt more like a best friend than a guy I was crushing on. I felt like I had known him forever, and the longer we were around each other, the more comfortable I became. The butterflies went away and I found myself stuttering less. I was opening up myself to him, allowing him to get to know the real Asia, the real me.

The first hour passed by quickly. It had felt more like a few minutes. I personally just wanted time to stand still so that I could stay right there, in that moment, forever. I don't want to sound all romance novel and fairytale desperate, but keep in mind that this was the first time in my life I had really just hung out with a dude. My past years had been running with a clique of females, one trying to outdo the next and compete with all the other girls at the same time. But right now, I'd forgotten about all of that. That was until I looked up to find Tracey stalked over me.

"I know it's been great for you being in La-La Land and all that, but are you ready to go back to the real world?" Tracey asked with much irritation as she shot me a mean glare.

I sat up, but Pierce pulled me back down.

"What are you doing?" I said, playfully shooing his hands off of me. "I have to go to second hour," I said to him with my hand on his chest.

"No you don't, ma," he said, but more like begged. I could hear a pinch of whininess in his voice.

Uh-oh, there goes that word again, I thought silently knowing that I liked the nickname he assigned me so much that I probably would have gotten it tattooed on my neck.

"Yes, I do. I don't need the school calling home telling my auntie that I was skipping," I said.

Tracey tapped her foot impatiently. "Look, are you coming or not, Asia?"

"She's staying here," Pierce answered Tracey for me, not taking his eyes off of me the entire time. "You never reported for your first class, so as long as you stay down here all day, the school won't call your house. They will just think you were absent today."

"Girl, don't let that boy have your aunt coming up here raising sand. Last year, anytime I wasn't at school by third period they were calling my house," Tracey said.

"Yeah, but that was because you were in middle school last year," Pierce reminded Tracey; bursting her Miss Know it All Bubble that had been floating over her head. "You in high school now, baby girl. They don't have to baby sit you here like they did last year." He looked at me to assure me that it wouldn't be a problem for me to hang out longer with him. "They'll just mark you absent today. They won't call your house until tomorrow, and that's only if you don't show up without a note explaining why you were absent today. Surely you know how to forge your aunt's handwriting." He then added, "Dang, girl, you ain't never ditched class before?"

Actually, I hadn't, but I didn't want him to think that I was some stuck-up, goody-two-shoes. I was far from that. So instead of answering his last question I just turned to Tracey, smiled and said, "I'm staying Tracey."

She shook her head and glared at me like I was her worst enemy in the world. "You are so out cold," she stated before stalking off.

"What was that all about?" Pierce asked.

"She likes you," I answered truthfully with a shrug of my shoulders. The shrug basically told him, "My best friend likes you, but I don't care.

"But I like you," he said bluntly while looking into my eyes. I felt like my world was moving in slow motion when he reached over and kissed me. "Do you like me?"

"You're alright," I stated with a confident smirk once the shock of the kiss wore off.

"Then it seems like your girl should be happy for you. If she's jealous or hating on you, then she doesn't seem like a good friend," he said.

I took his words to heart and thought that he had a point. Tracey was hating, but she was my best friend and I decided that I would hash out my beef with her later.

As the basement eventually began to clear out, the people leaving included the cheerleaders. Miranda gave me an extra harsh look as she walked by slowly, but then softened her facial expression when she looked over at Pierce.

"Bye, Pierce." Miranda put her hand up to her mouth and ear as if it was a telephone. "Call me later, okay?" she stated, letting me know that he had her number.

She thought she was being slick or getting underneath my skin, but she was wrong. Obviously he wasn't stressing her because he was hugged up with me right in her face, so I smirked and replied, "I'll make sure I remind him before he hangs up with me. Bye now." I waved my fingers and gave her a false smile.

She looked at Pierce as if he was supposed to defend her. All he did was look back at her and say, "She said she'll remind me." He then turned his attention to me as if telling her to kick bricks.

Her friends snickered and she stormed off with her arms folded. That was two chicks in the past few minutes that had stormed away at the sight of Pierce and me together. One I knew for a fact Pierce had no ties to. The other one was a different story that I felt I needed to get to the bottom of before things got more serious with this guy than they were already getting.

"But Miranda's not your girlfriend, huh?" I said sarcastically.

"Nope, I'm staring at my girlfriend right now," he responded sweetly while looking into my eyes.

Ooooh, I hated that this boy had so much game. I could see already that he was going to have me wrapped around his finger. I smiled as I thought of going to homecoming and prom with him.

He leaned in again and we kissed for what felt like hours. That day in the basement we got to know each other and I officially became his girl . . . just like that. No dating, no first talking on the phone until wee hours in the night. It was just an instant connection that couldn't be denied.

I knew me having a boyfriend was going to be a problem with my aunt Joy, but Pierce was a charmer. He seemed nice enough. After all, he didn't appear to have any enemies. Everyone liked him. And in my plight to be "That Chick," I knew that just off the strength of his popularity, I would become the most popular girl at Cass. So basically, I was killing two birds with one stone. I was getting my man, plus my popularity. That did not necessarily mean that I was going to be well liked, just well known.

Pierce and I stayed down in the basement, talking, cuddling and kissing until we heard the last school bell ring. I was so engrossed in him that I barely realized it was time to go. I didn't want to go. I never thought I would say it, but I could have stayed at school forever (as long as it was down in the basement with Pierce).

"I've got to go," I said as I stood up and straightened out my clothes. "I have to hurry up and catch my bus home. I wouldn't want to miss it again, now would I?" I joked.

"Missing your bus wasn't actually a bad thing after all," Pierce said as he stood.

"Hmmmm," I teased for a minute. "I guess not." Missing my bus had been fate. No telling if Pierce and I would be together right now if I hadn't.

"Let me take you home," he said.

"I told you, you can't," I replied.

"Doesn't your aunt work? Let me take you home. I promise I'll be gone before she gets there," he said.

I don't know if it was because of his charm or my own stupidity, but I agreed and the next thing I knew we were in his car and he was headed towards my crib. Everybody in my school was surprised to see us together. The way that he held onto my hand let everyone know that we were an official couple. When he pulled up to my house I hurriedly got out of the car.

"Can I come in?" he asked.

"No," I said. "You don't know my auntie Joy. I can't take that chance. She could have neighbors reporting to her for all I know."

"Just for a minute? I promise, I'll be out before the hour is even over," he promised with his hand on his heart. "Come on, ma, don't break my heart. The longer we stay out here is the less time we have in there." He convinced me just that easily.

"Come on," I invited as I backpedaled away from the car. "Park your car a couple spaces down and come through the back door. We got some nosy neighbors."

He nodded and I went into the house. A couple minutes later he was knocking at the back door. I answered it and he rushed in, kissing me as he maneuvered his way inside. One would have thought that we hadn't just spent the entire day together. It was crazy how he was making me feel. It wasn't my first kiss. I had kissed a couple of boys before, but the feeling was nothing like this. This was much more intense and it made me feel grown up. *This must be why my Auntie Joy is so afraid for me to experience sex. This feels so good,* I thought as he kissed my neck. *It can't feel much better than this.* Pierce tried to reach underneath my shirt and I snapped back to reality.

I grabbed his hands. "Stop," I whispered.

"Are you a virgin?" he asked. This boy did not beat around the bush, that's for sure.

"Yeah, I am," I replied in embarrassment. With any other guy I would have probably lied my butt off and just made them think that I didn't want to get down with them, but Pierce wasn't just any other guy. He was a guy I really liked and I didn't want to hurt his feelings by making him think that I didn't want to be with him. I also didn't want him to think that I was just some tease, because, here I was all day long acting all experienced and fast, when in actuality I did not know what I was doing. I did know that the situation was moving way too quickly for me. I had to slow things down with Pierce and make him move at my pace, but honestly I knew that I would not be able to keep him for long if I wasn't giving it up.

He sighed deeply, but didn't say anything.

"Are you mad?" I asked.

"No, I ain't mad. I didn't know you were a virgin though," he said. "I wouldn't have asked you to be my girl."

"What?" I snapped. Just that quickly it was like the fairytale was over. The prince had turned into a toad. "You act like that's a bad thing. At least I'm not one of those busted nasty girls."

"I know, ma, and I like you, but I'm too attracted to you. You're so sexy that when I'm around you I can't stop myself from touching you," he said. I didn't know whether or not this boy was running game on me, but I ate it all up. I was actually flattered by what he was saying. "Are you saving yourself for when you get married?"

I shrugged. "I don't know, I haven't really thought about it. I just haven't done it yet. I guess I haven't found the person I want to give it to," I admitted.

"What about me?" he asked as he kissed my lips, confusing me and distracting me all at the same time.

"I mean I don't know you that well yet," I said, trying my best to stay focused and not getting caught up in a web of words.

"You can get to know me. I know that I like you, but I want you to trust me enough to give me that. I want to be with you . . . all of you. You're special to me," he said. "Haven't I proven to you just how special you are to me? He kissed me softly on the lips. "You wanna be my girl, right?"

"Yeah I do," I said. Right about now, it was hard telling that I was the older of us two. I felt like a freshman girl infatuated by an older boy, kind of what Tracey was probably feeling like. Only the boy really did like me just as much as I liked him.

I hadn't even officially been his woman a good twenty-four hours, and I didn't want my being a virgin to be the reason why he broke up with me so soon. That would definitely lose me some cool points. So I made up my mind then and there that I would not make him wait forever. He was going to be my first. It was the price that I had to pay to be his girlfriend, and the most popular girl at school.

The way I saw it, I did not really have a choice. I knew how the game went. The minute I didn't give Pierce what he wanted, there would be a line of girls waiting to take my place, and I was not going to have that. No way was I going to spend the rest of my high school days as the chick who couldn't keep her man.

Even though my aunt Joy had told me over and over how she felt about me, sex and boys, at this moment, I didn't' care. I had to do it if I wanted to keep him. I made myself feel better by telling myself over and over again that everybody else my age had probably already started having sex. I don't know for sure if any of the girls I used to roll with had done it or not, because like I said before, sex had never really been the topic of our conversations. It was my aunt Joy who all of a sudden made me take a double look at the issue. And now it seemed as though she had opened up a brand new can of worms.

As Pierce stood there kissing all over me, peer pressure became my biggest motivation to just go ahead and go all the way, so I gave in and led Pierce to my room. As we walked hand in hand, I'm surprised mine didn't slip right out of his it was so sweaty. And let's not even talk about the knot in my stomach. My heart was beating out of my chest and I felt like I wanted to cry. Everything inside of me screamed for me to turn around and send Pierce packing if he couldn't deal with the fact that I wasn't ready yet, but I had already told him yes. Adding the label of a "tease" on top of everything else was far too much for a teenage girl to bear. I could not back out now. It was too late.

After entering my bedroom, I closed the door behind us. He undressed me and his hands ran all over my body. What he was doing felt good to me, but I was also afraid. I had heard different stories through other girls around my old neighborhood.

Some had said that their first time was painful; others said it was the best time of their life. So far I only had one word to describe what I was going through and that was unsure. I was unsure about the entire thing. I knew I wasn't ready, but I wanted to please Pierce. My goal was to keep him happy and interested in me. It was the reason I told him yes.

He unsnapped my bra and I felt a tear slide from my eye. Right before I felt his hands making their way up to my breast I opened my mouth to say no. I thought I could go through with this whole thing, but I couldn't. I'd just have to suffer the consequences whatever they may be. Before the word 'no' could even make its way up my throat and onto my tongue, the sound of a slamming door halted the entire show.

"Asia?" I heard my aunt call out.

"Oh shoot! That's my aunt! She's home!" I yelled and pushed Pierce away from me.

"I thought she was at work!" he whispered.

"She is . . . I mean, I thought she was . . . I mean, she was supposed to be," I stammered as I began to scramble for my clothes. In the midst of trying to get dressed, I realized that my main concern should be getting rid of Pierce. "Here, go out of the window," I said as I pushed him towards it while snapping on my bra.

"Okay, call me tonight," he whispered as he kissed my cheek and disappeared.

I fumbled to get all of my articles of clothing back on. Last but not least I managed to get my shirt on. I quickly buttoned it up and rushed out into the hallway, nearly bumping my auntie over as I crashed directly into her.

"What is the rush? Didn't you hear me calling you? What are you doing up here?" she asked me, suspiciously looking over my shoulder and into my bedroom.

My mind could not find an answer for her quick enough, and I began to stammer. "I umm, I was umm . . ."

"Girl, what is wrong with you!" Auntie Joy snapped, pushing past me and peeking inside my room. After seeing for herself that everything was in order, she turned around and faced me. "Get down there to do your chores," she fussed. "I knew you didn't do nothing but mess around when you got home from school. Probably wait until I'm on my way home to start cleaning. But I caught you off guard today, didn't I? Umm, hmm, my shift ended early today, too many nurses for the few patients." She scanned the house like it was a pig sty or something. "You've been home for nearly an hour and you haven't done anything yet. I really need you to step up and be more responsible, Asia. You are not a little girl anymore."

I scanned the house too, not looking for dirt, though. Instead, I was looking for any evidence that Pierce might have left behind that gave away the fact that a boy had been in the house. I was relieved to see that he hadn't. "I know, ma'am, and I'm sorry," I said. In all actuality, the house didn't even look that bad, but I was not about to start nothing.

Words can't even describe how glad I was that the only thing Auntie Joy was fussing about was the house. My heart finally returned to its normal pace as I crept past my aunt and went to complete my chores. This was the first time I had done the chores happily and with a smile. And it was also the first time I had ever welcomed Auntie Joy and her fussing. I was grateful for Auntie Joy's interruption. She had actually saved me from giving in to Pierce. I did like him, but I had been scared. *I just need a little bit more time before we take it that far,* I thought as I absentmindedly went through my normal routine.

I had gotten out of going all the way with him this time around, but what about the next time, which I'm sure there would be. I needed some advice, and I needed it fast, before I hooked up with Pierce again. The only person I could think of to call was Tracey. I knew I could tell her everything. We had shared all kinds of secrets with each other and had given each other sound advice. I needed her to tell me what I should do. She may have been younger than me, but with the experiences of all of her older siblings, she knew a lot about life.

I sped through my chores at supersonic speed, and as soon as I was done, I took the phone to my room, shutting the door so that I could have some privacy. I dialed Tracey's phone number and she picked up and greeted me on the second ring. Well, I guess you could call it a greeting.

"Well, well, well. If it ain't my used to be best friend," Tracey stated. She never answered any calls until she screened them first with the caller ID, so I knew she would know it was me.

"What? Why are you tripping? What is up with you?" I asked, trying to play nonchalant. Maybe if I acted as though things weren't that serious, then she would too.

"You know what's good, Asia. You are always trying to play Miss Goody Goody. You knew I liked Pierce and you backstabbed me by going after him yourself. You ain't slick. You stole him right from underneath my nose you fake bit . . ."

"Stole him?" I said, cutting her off. "Technically, he talked to me first!"

"Yeah, let you tell it. But I know the real deal," Tracey said in a knowing tone. "He probably did come up to you to talk to you, but it was so that he could juice you for information about me. But I could see you know stealing the spotlight, because we both know how much you like the spotlight. It probably drove you crazy that someone like him could be interested in me over you," Tracey spoke as if what she was saying was Bible.

I wanted to tell that girl that she had watched one too many after school specials over the years, but what good would it have done. Her mind was made up about Pierce, and if it made her feel any better, then what was the harm in letting her think it?

"Look, Tracey, I'm sorry about everything, but right now I really need your advice on something."

"Does this something have anything to do with Pierce?"

I sighed. "You are my best friend. I was going to

let you have him, Tracey, but he came back at me," I defended.

"Whatever, Asia. What do you want? My grandmother needs me to run to the store for her."

I knew she was rushing me off the phone, but I thought for sure that after she heard what I had to say she would make time to talk to me. "I almost had sex with Pierce today," I whispered, making sure Auntie Joy didn't hear me.

"You did what?" she asked. I couldn't tell if she was shocked or pissed.

"I almost had sex with him. I told him yes, but my aunt came home and he had to leave. I don't know if I should do it or not. I'm supposed to call him tonight," I said. "Should I do it?"

"So he tried to get at you like that already?" Tracey asked. I could tell by her tone what she was thinking. She thought that Pierce was only trying to get at me for one thing. I could tell by her voice that she almost wanted to laugh at me. But I didn't say anything. I knew it was the furthest thing from the truth. But if it made her feel even that much better to think that was all Pierce wanted from me, and if allowing her to think that was going to get our friendship back on the right track again, then so be it.

"Yes, he did," I confirmed. "And I know eventually he's going to want to pick up where we left off. So should I?"

Without hesitating, Tracey replied, "Yeah, go ahead. Everybody does it."

"Have you?" I inquired. Like I said, we'd never really talked about sex.

"Girl, yeah. I'm surprised you waited this long to have sex," she said as if I should be ashamed of myself for still being a virgin. "But then again maybe it will be worth the wait since it looks like your first will be with the most popular dude at school. Girl, I would do it if I were you," she stated.

"You would?" I questioned again with uncertainty. "I mean, you ain't gon' trip that my first is Pierce? Supposedly the boy you liked?"

"Don't remind me, Asia," she jokingly warned.

"Thanks, girl. I just needed to talk to somebody to make sure I'm not making a mistake. Tracey, I really do like him," I admitted with a small smile.

"Yeah, yeah, yeah," she said in a sing-song voice. I imagined her playfully swooshing her hand to brush me off. "I will get at you tomorrow. Like I said, I have to go to the store. Peace." She hung up before I got the chance to say bye.

I knew underneath it all, she was still just a little

salty over the fact that I was the one that Pierce had chosen, but I figured if she wasn't completely over it already, she would get over it eventually. She had to, because it looked like Pierce and I were about to be an item. It's not like I was putting a dude before my girl, because I wanted to be down with the both of them. Of course, now I wanted to do a little bit more than just be down with Pierce.

Tracey was a good friend and had always been there for me. Just the simple fact that she had told me to go through with losing my virginity to Pierce let me know that it was okay to follow her advice. She'd never steered me wrong before. Like she said, everyone was doing it. I did not want to be the only one left out.

Chapter Four

The next day when I arrived at my bus stop, Pierce was waiting there for me in his car. Instead of getting on the bus, I hopped into his car and sat proudly as I rode shot gun. We pulled into the student parking lot and I slowly got out so that everybody standing around outside could see Pierce and me together. Envy was so thick in the air that I could darn near smell it. I walked side by side with Pierce, his arm was draped over my shoulders casually, but the interaction between us let everyone know what was up. I was marked as his girl, so no other guys could try to get at me. I was proudly taken.

"I thought about what happened with us last night," I whispered nervously in his ear. We had managed to avoid the subject matter the entire ride to school.

"Oh yeah?" he replied. "What have you been thinking?"

"That I want to," I stated.

He stopped walking for a moment. "Straight up? You sure?" he asked and then started walking again.

"Yeah, I'm sure, but we can't do it at my house, that's for sure. My aunt's schedule is too unpredictable. I don't want her to walk in on us," I answered.

"Don't worry, I'll take care of that," he replied. He leaned down and kissed my cheek then we parted to go to our separate classes.

On my way to class I stopped off real quick at Tracey's locker. "Hey girl," I greeted as she was finishing up at her locker.

She threw up a peace sign after closing her locker. I frowned at the nonchalant gesture. We were always happy to see each other, but today, all of a sudden, she had a stank attitude. I thought after our phone conversation last night, everything was back on point with us. Maybe I'd thought wrong.

"What's wrong with you?" I asked.

"I'm chilling. Ain't nothing wrong. I just don't feel like being all up in nobody's face," she replied as she turned to head to her own class.

I knew she was trying to be funny. It took everything in me to keep my cool. I was ready to go off on Tracey, but I gave her a pass and ignored her. "I spotted you and Pierce walking into the building all arm in arm. So what, are you two like together now?"

"Oh so now you're talking to me?" I asked playfully. I smiled and waited for her response as I slowly walked a couple of paces behind her.

"I was just asking," Tracey said as if it did not matter.

"Why are you mad at me? Is this about Pierce again?" I already knew that it was about Pierce, but I wanted to put all of my cards on the table. "I thought we'd squashed this yesterday." Evidently, Tracey seeing me with Pierce this morning had caused her attitude to resurface.

"I'm not mad at anybody. I just still think it's kind of messed up how you went after the boy that I liked," Tracey said.

"Okay, for real, let's put it out there on the table." Both Tracey and I stopped walking. She turned to face me as I continued. "I really like Pierce. Please don't trip about this. You're my girl. I have enough people hating on me already. I don't need my supposed to be best friend to jump on that bandwagon too."

"Hating?"

"Come on, Tracey, you know I did not mean it like that. I just want everything to be cool. Are we good?"

Tracey shrugged. "Yeah we're good. I told you I'm not mad. Pierce is on yesterday's agenda." She changed the subject, but not really. "Why weren't you on the bus today? Did your aunt drop you off at school?"

"Pierce picked me up today," I said with a smirk. I knew that it would get underneath her skin, but I did not care. I had always supported her, so I expected her to get over herself and be there for me.

"Well, I've gotta go. Have a good day," she said as she walked off and into her classroom.

As I made my way to my class, I could feel people looking at me. Some people had envy in their eyes, while others went out of their way to speak to me.

Running with a popular clique of girls like I'd done in the past had nothing on being Pierce's girlfriend. Being his girl was like being teen royalty. Suddenly everybody knew my name and wanted to be around me. I was the center of attention at lunch. I had more friends than I had ever had. I was a permanent fixture on Pierce's arm. We were the cutest couple in school and high school at Cass was everything it could have possibly been and more.

Over time, Tracey remained distant, but she had chilled with the sarcastic comments. We were not as close as we once were, but I had a new boyfriend and really did not have a lot of time for anything else but him anyway. Auntie Joy knew nothing about me having a boyfriend, but I snuck around so that I could see Pierce. I began to skip class with Pierce almost every day, and what was once the upper class hangout spot in the basement, became Pierce's and my private spot.

I did not think I was wrong for lying to my aunt about my whereabouts when I was with Pierce. I felt like he would keep me safe and I would do anything to spend time with him. I would tell my aunt that I was with Tracey, but in actuality I would be with Pierce, going to the movies or just hanging out. It got to the point where he was the most important thing in my life. Tracey, school, family . . . none of it mattered more than him. I don't know if I was clinging to him because my father was no longer in my life, but I knew that Pierce made me feel accepted and important.

Homecoming was coming up and I was excited about going. Pierce and I had already decided that our color would be blue, so all I had to do was find a cute blue dress. He could not pick me up for the dance because my aunt had made it clear about how she felt about boys, period. I didn't want to open a can of worms with her, so to avoid any unnecessary drama and explaining, I told Pierce that I would meet him at the dance.

I had a fairytale image of how I wanted homecoming to go. I knew that I would feel like a princess that night and I was lucky to share it with my prince charming. Auntie Joy scraped up enough money to buy me a royal blue, satin, spaghetti strap dress. It was backless and lay over my curves as if it had been made especially for me. It was sexy and made me look older, which is why I liked it. I did not want to feel like a kid on that day. My dress made me feel grown and I was sure that I would be the best dressed girl at the dance.

The night of the dance came quickly. I was nervous and had first date jitters as I closed my eyes and let Auntie Joy apply my make-up.

"Are you excited?" she asked sweetly, standing before me in her nurses scrubs. She had to go into work, but had managed to trade shifts at work with someone in order to be able to be home to help me get ready.

"Yeah I am," I admitted. "It's my first dance. This is the first time I've dressed up like this. I wish my daddy was here with me." It was sentimental times like this that I missed him most. Sometimes a girl just wanted her father to be around. I felt like I was being robbed of something because he wasn't here.

"He is here with you, Asia," Auntie Joy replied. "He is always with you and he is looking down on you right now. I know my brother and he would not miss this moment for the world. You look beautiful and your father sees you."

I smiled and nodded. I let her words hit my heart because I needed to hear them. I really hoped that her words were true.

"I'm sorry I have to work tonight, but I hope you have a wonderful time. Your curfew is midnight, and not a minute later, Asia," she said as she closed her make-up kit and kissed my cheek. "I love you, babe."

"I love you too," I replied. "Don't worry about me. I'll be fine. I will tell you all about the dance tomorrow."

"I can't wait to hear all about it," she said.

I smiled at that rare moment of closeness between my aunt and me. She left the house and minutes later I was right behind her. I called Tracey, who had gotten her older brother Damian to drive us to the dance. They came and picked me up.

"You look good, girl," I complimented. Her ivory dress was cocktail length and had a baby doll fit. She looked cute.

"I know," she answered without commenting on my dress.

She didn't have to tell me how I looked though. Just the fact that she went out of her way not to give me my props let me know that my stuff was on point. She was becoming a first class hater.

After I got in the car, Damian glanced in the backseat and nodded his head at me. "What up, Asia?" he greeted. "You look good, baby."

I blushed and replied, "Thanks." I had always had a huge crush on him, but he was six years older than me, so I knew that he was off limits, but it did not stop me from looking.

When we arrived at the school, there were cars and even limos pulling up left and right. I got out of the car and immediately found Pierce, who was waiting for me at the entrance. His eyes scanned my body and I knew he was pleased with my appearance.

"Wow," he said.

"Wow to yourself," I replied as I admired his black tuxedo.

We went inside, linked by the hip and hit the dance floor. We danced for hours; clowning and having fun with all of our classmates. I felt so special. I knew that I would never get another night like that night. The décor of the room, the elegance of it all; it overwhelmed me and I decided that it was the night for me to fulfill my end of the bargain with Pierce. It was the night that we would take our relationship to the next level. All he had to do was answer one question correctly.

"Thank you for asking me to homecoming," I said as we took a break from dancing and sipped on punch.

"Who else was I going to ask? You're my girl. Everybody knows that," he replied.

"I know. I just know that you could have chosen anybody and you chose me, so I wanted to thank you for that. You mean a lot to me," I admitted. "I think I might love you or at least like you a whole lot," I said it in a joking way so that he would not think I was taking things too quickly.

"I love you too ma," he replied.

"Do you?" I asked in complete shock. I hadn't expected him to return the sentiment, although I was hoping he would.

"I said it, didn't I?" he asked. I smiled and nodded.

Just then Usher's latest slow jam came on and we made our way back to the dance floor.

"I have a surprise for you," I replied as I draped my arms around his neck.

"Yeah?"

"Yeah," I assured him confidently. "I want to give you something."

"What's that?" he asked.

"You know," I answered with a quick kiss on the lips. "We got interrupted the first time we tried. We won't this time."

"Are you talking about what I think you're talking about?" he asked. "Are you sure?"

I nodded and put my head into his chest shyly. "You love me, right?"

"I already told you I do," he said.

"Then I'm sure," I replied.

He grabbed my hand and led me off of the dance floor. "Where are we going?" I asked as I looked around to see if anyone had noticed us leaving.

"Shh, just follow me," he replied.

I trusted him, so I followed him quietly out of the gym, through the darkened hallways, and down into the closed off basement that had become our personal hideout spot. "What are we doing down here?" I asked. "We're missing the dance."

"You said you were sure," he reminded me.

"What? You want to do it down here? Now?" I asked. I looked around the cold, darkened area. There were old school desks and chairs littered throughout the room. It was dusty and I could hardly see Pierce, even though he was standing right in front of my face. This was not the place I had envisioned when I thought of losing my virginity. It wasn't romantic or intimate at all. I pictured a nice hotel room fixed with all the perks you see on TV, when a couple is about to have sex. Where were the flowers? What about the rose petals? Where were the candles? It wasn't supposed to happen in a dreary basement. I was about to give up something that I had held onto for seventeen years and

I had expected my first time to be a little bit more luxurious than what was before me.

"Why not now?" he asked.

I didn't respond, but my eyes scanned the room once more in doubt. I was skeptical and disappointed that it was about to go down like this, but I couldn't tell him no, so I put up a front, and when he kissed me, I kissed him back. The feeling of his lips made my heart race and I forgot that just a couple minutes ago I was reluctant to go through with our plans.

I liked Pierce. Sometimes I even felt that I really loved him, although most adults would say that I knew nothing about love. I hated when grown-ups tried to look down on young people and tried to tell them how to feel or what to think. I'm old enough to know what's up and I was sure that what I had with Pierce would last forever. He was my boyfriend and I had already mapped out our entire future together. I would sit in class writing down wedding plans, naming all of my friends and his friends, along with our wedding color scheme.

I had it all envisioned in my head. When I graduated and went off to college, like I knew my aunt would make me do, we would keep in touch through email and phone calls. I would try to sneak away to see him when I could, but would wait faithfully until I was able to come back for holiday breaks. It would be hard for a minute, but when he graduated, he would apply to the same college as I was attending and we would finally be reunited.

I imagined all of these things as he undressed me; slipping the straps of my dress off my shoulders. I was shy and insecure about my body. I knew that I was attractive and had a nice shape, but I wasn't used to anyone besides myself seeing me naked on a regular, and now I stood before him, once again, as bare as the day I was born.

Almost like the last time, though, he didn't seem to notice, because he was too anxious about the next step. He took of his tux jacket and laid it down on the ground. When we lay down on the basement floor I began to have second thoughts. My body tensed up, and what I thought would be pleasure was actually a great amount of pain.

"Oww," I whispered. "Wait."

He stopped and looked at me in irritation. "You want me to stop?" he asked. From the tone of his voice I knew that he was losing his patience. I did not want him to break up with me and I did not want to take away something that I had already promised him he could have, so instead of doing what I wanted to do, which was stop, I shook my head and told him to keep going. *Just get it over with. You love him and he loves you. He deserves this,* I told myself. He was my prince and what we had was a fairytale. I wasn't going to be the one to ruin it by telling him no.

I felt like I was being ripped apart and my body tensed up. My legs shook uncontrollably and I stifled my tears. It hurt so badly and I wondered why girls had told me that their first time had been good. I silently wondered if something was wrong with me, and I blocked out the pain until eventually it faded away. After only a few minutes I was lying on the cold floor and Pierce was adjusting his clothes. The next thing I knew, there was a sudden flash of light. He had pulled out his cell phone and was aiming his camera at me.

"Smile for me, sexy. I want a picture of my girlfriend," he instructed. I covered up as best as I could and gave him my best bright white smile.

"You feel a'ight?" he asked.

I nodded and sat up to get dressed. The drip drop of the leaky basement was not what I had fantasized about and I wished that my first time could have been more special, but it was too late for that. I had already gone through with it. I had nothing left to lose, but somehow I felt a little bit older . . . a bit more mature; even though I was only a little girl playing a grown woman's role.

I was shaking, but didn't know if it was a result of the temperature or the fact that I had just taken my body through something that it was not ready for. Either way, I felt like I was weak. "I think I just need to lie down. Can you take me home?" I asked.

He agreed and gave me his suit jacket for me to wear as we made our way up the steps and out the front of the building. He gave my hand a squeeze of reassurance and leaned down to whisper in my ear. "You're my world, girl."

Those words touched my heart and I smiled sheepishly. He cared about me, and at that moment, any doubt that I had conjured was erased by the affection that he showed me.

He ended up dropping me off at the corner of my street and I walked the rest of the way. I didn't want Auntie Joy to catch me getting out of a boy's car. She would have had a fit and probably would have been sniffing my panties to make sure I hadn't done the unthinkable. Little did she know, the 'crime' had already been committed and there was nothing for her to protect anymore.

I knew that she would never understand. I loved

Pierce and I felt like what we had would last forever, but I knew that she would think that I was young and dumb. No, it was best for me to hide it from her and continue to see Pierce secretly. Besides, our business didn't belong to anyone but us. She did not need to know, unless I wanted her to. I ran my fingers through my long, curled, hair to make sure that everything was in place before I walked into the house, a totally different girl than I had been when I'd walked out of it.

Chapter Five

Auntie Joy had dozed off on the sofa. She was still dressed in her work clothes. I smiled because she was expertly balancing a Newport cigarette in her left hand even though she was knocked out. I leaned over her and kissed her cheek.

"I'm home, Auntie," I said.

She reluctantly opened her eyes, hit a puff of her square, and stretched her arms out. "Oh, hi, baby. How was the dance, baby?" she asked as the cigarette smoke escaped through her lips with each word.

"It was good," I answered. "I had fun. It was a whole lotta fun. Me and Tracey did it up real big." I paused for a minute. "What are you doing home? I thought you traded shifts and had to be at work."

She sat up on the couch. "I did go to work. It's just that they didn't even have me down at all. I got home not too long ago. I would have been home earlier, but an emergency came in that I had to help tend to first." She looked over at the clock on the wall that hung above the television. "Never mind what I'm doing home. Why are you home so early? I thought you all were going out to eat afterwards," she stated when she noticed that it was only eleven thirty.

"We were, but I started cramping," I lied quickly and a little bit too easily for comfort. I was getting good at making her believe what I wanted her too. I didn't like the fact that I had to lie to her, but Pierce was worth it. "I just came home right after the dance."

"Okay, well there is some Midol in the medicine cabinet upstairs. Go take a hot bath, it may help you feel better. I'll put some hot tea on your night stand," she said in a motherly way.

I smiled and nodded, then headed towards the bathroom. I needed to take a shower anyway. I felt dirty, and sticky. I showered quickly, scrubbing down every inch of my body. Afterwards I retired to my room, where just as Auntie Joy promised, there was a cup of hot tea at my bed side. I picked up the mug and took a sip, allowing the hot beverage to flow down my throat and through my body. I looked over at the clock. Only fifteen minutes had passed. Tracey had told her brother to pick us up after the dance. Surely he'd picked her up and she was home by now, unless she went out to eat anyway, even though I had dipped out.

I grabbed the phone and dialed Tracey's cell phone instead of her home number. Knowing her, I figured that she was probably still out, but I couldn't' wait to share my news with her. I just had to tell somebody what had happened to me that night. When Tracey answered, I could hear chatter in the background.

"Hey, girl, where are you?" I asked.

"Everybody went to Fishbones after the dance. Where are you? I tried to wait on you, but you were taking forever and I didn't see Pierce, so I figured you left with him," she said.

"I did leave with him." I covered my mouth and the phone receiver and then whispered into the phone, "We did it."

"Did it?" she asked. Then as if a light bulb suddenly went off in her head she exclaimed, "Oooh! Did it! Say you swear!"

I laughed. "I swear on everything I love. It was

just like you said it would be . . . good." It was another lie, but I couldn't possible tell her that my first time had been painful, unromantic, and nothing like I'd imagined it would be. "But I will fill you in on everything tomorrow. I've gotta go before my auntie hears me. Have fun."

"Oh don't worry I will," she said before disconnecting the call.

I drank the rest of my tea, then I laid down. A smile managed to creep on my face. Although my first time hadn't gone anything like I thought it would, at least it had been with Pierce. Knowing that kept a smile on my face until I drifted off to sleep.

The next couple of days I tried to get a hold of Tracey, but she was never available or didn't pick up her cell phone. I figured she'd over done it at the dance and was recuperating.

Come Monday morning, I couldn't wait to get on the school bus and chat it up with Tracey on the way to school, but when I got on the bus, Tracey wasn't there. I figured she had overslept and was going to get a ride from her older brother. I couldn't wait to finish telling her about my night at the dance. It had been killing me not being able to talk about it to anyone.

As soon as I got to school I waited for her at the entrance to the school. It was almost time for the first bell to ring and she still hadn't arrived. I wanted to see Pierce before I had to report to class. I figured she wasn't coming, so I eventually went inside. I saw Pierce up the hall and I called his name.

"Pierce!" I yelled out as I waved my hand.

He turned towards me and gave me a head nod before continuing to walk in the opposite direction with his friends in tow. I frowned. He usually came and walked me to class. We usually graced the hallways as the cutest couple in school, but since I had waited outside for Tracey for so long, I just assumed that he didn't want to be late for class.

I'll catch up with him after class, I thought as I jogged up the stairs to my first hour class. I was almost inside my class when I heard the late bell ring. "Dang!" I yelled aloud as I stopped running and took my time getting inside the classroom. There wasn't a use in rushing now. I was already tardy. I sauntered into the class and immediately took my seat. My teacher looked up from his desk.

"You're late, Asia," he stated sternly.

"I know. I had to stop at my locker to get my books," I responded, adding another lie to my long list of falsehoods.

"She was probably in the basement!" somebody from the back of the room mumbled loudly in between coughs.

"Yeah, probably looking for her panties," another added.

I thought I was going to lose my breakfast right there on the floor when I heard some giggling take place after the comment. I knew exactly what that little comment meant, and obviously, so did everyone else.

I was appalled and couldn't believe that the word had gotten out somehow about Pierce and me. But how could they have known? Surely Pierce wouldn't have played me like that, and no one else knew, no one except Tracey. A look of disbelief covered my face. I couldn't believe that she had told everybody about me having sex with Pierce. It took everything in me to sit there in class and focus. My attention was on the clock. I couldn't wait for first period to end so that I could get with Miss Best Friend.

First hour seemed like first two hours, but eventually the period ended and I headed straight to Tracey's locker.

"Did you tell anybody?" I whispered harshly to her as I stood next to her locker.

She snickered through her nose. “I didn’t have too,” she replied snottily with a roll of her eyes. “Look, I’m late. Gotta go.” And just like that she was off to her next class. Unfortunately, I was off to my next class, to face a whole new group of people who probably knew my business too.

Second hour ticked by slowly. I felt like I was sitting inside a closet with all eyes on me. I heard the snickers and the sarcastic comments. I wished that a hole would just come, swallow me up and take me away from it all. I was embarrassed. Suddenly I felt more insecure than I ever had in my entire life. It was as if everybody knew what had happened between Pierce and me. Tracey had denied putting my business out, but I knew deep down that she was the one who had spread it all over the school. I just hoped that the word hadn’t spread any further, like to the teachers, and then even worse, to my Auntie Joy.

At that moment I felt like the only person I could trust was Pierce. I wished we were in the same grade so that I could talk to him. I needed to see him as soon as possible. Sitting there for sixty minutes was torture. I could barely breathe and I did not hear one word my teacher said. When the bell finally freed me, I sprang out of my seat. I passed Tracey in the hall and noticed the smug look on her face. At that moment I could have killed her, but I had already wasted enough time on her this morning. I needed to see Pierce.

I rushed to Pierce's locker to find him standing there with a group of upperclassmen. They were all huddled around him, even Miranda and the other cheerleaders were peering over his shoulder making comments.

"Hey," I said as I made my way through the crowd. I tapped his shoulder and he turned towards me. "I need to talk to you." By this time I had tears in my eyes. I just wanted him to take me away from all of this. As long as I had him, I was good. I didn't care about anything or anybody else. I wanted him to make me feel better about the situation.

"What about, ma? I'm busy right now," he replied.

I looked up at him in confusion. He had never brushed me off the way that he was now, and I got the feeling that he was mad at me or something. Perhaps he'd already heard about our business being out there. Even worse, because I hadn't gotten a chance to talk to him all morning, he probably thought that I was dodging him because I had something to do with it. I had to make things right, and fast.

"I need to talk to you Pierce. I need you right now." My voice trembled, but I contained my emotions. "I have to talk to you, Pierce, it's important." I managed to get the words out without breaking down in tears.

"Dang! Why are you all in my man's face?" I heard Miranda say as she slid next to Pierce and he put his arm around her shoulders.

"Your man?!" I yelled before looking at Pierce for some answers.

"I'll get at you later, Asia. We'll hook up . . . when I need some more of what you gave me at the dance," he stated arrogantly.

"Me, too," one of his boys added. "I hear you give one heck of a slow dance."

His crowd of friends laughed at my expense and I ran into the girl's bathroom. I was heated. I couldn't believe he had just played me out in front of the entire school. Even the girls who were already in the bathroom were looking at me funny.

"What are y'all skanks looking at?" I yelled.

"The only skank in here is you. You're the one getting busted out in the basement," a girl replied before leaving.

I leaned over the sink and let my tears flow. This could not be happening to me. How had the entire school found out about this? Another girl came out of one of the stalls and stood uncomfortably behind me as she watched me bawl. I was too ashamed to even look up, but I could feel her standing there. I just buried my face in my hands and cried.

"Excuse me," she said as she maneuvered around me to wash her hands.

An uncomfortable silence occupied the space between us, I could feel her staring, but I did not care. "So I guess you know too, huh?" I asked without looking up at her.

"Yeah, I know," the girl replied. "I knew what was going to happen when you first started hollering at Pierce. He's just like every other high school dude in this school. The only reason why he even talked to you is because he knows about all you've gone through and he wanted to take advantage of you." I heard the water run for a second and then it stopped. Next I heard the ripping sound of a paper towel. "But you know, I betted against you falling for the okey doke. I mean last year, you were one of the girls that I envied. You seemed strong willed and like you had it all. I guess losing a loved one can sometimes cause you to lose yourself. Trust me, I know. Looks like you got caught up in Pierce's popularity. Believe me, you ain't the first one he done pulled that crap on and you won't be the last."

I sniffled aloud, not ashamed to be crying my eyes out, but too ashamed to look up and see her watching me do it. "I just don't know how everybody knows. The only other person who knew was my friend, Tracey," I admitted. I don't know why I was in the bathroom sharing my life story with this girl. I guess she was the only person who was willing to talk to me and I needed to talk to somebody.

Still not making eye contact with the girl, I heard her fiddle around in her purse and then pull out something. "Look. This is how everybody knows. I got this over the weekend," she said.

I opened my eyes to be staring at her cell phone. It showed me the picture that Pierce had taken of me at the dance down in the basement right after we had done it. It had been forwarded to her phone with a message that read: *While everybody else was dancing in the gym, Pierce was hitting this in the school basement. If you want it, she will give it to you. Forward this to ten friends so someone else can get lucky too.*

I put my hand over my mouth and closed my eyes as I continued to sob. "Your girl didn't tell everybody," the girl said. "Pierce did. All he wanted to do from jump was to humiliate you."

I was stunned. "But he said he loved me," I said, shaking my head from side to side in complete disbelief.

"Look, I know you are young and you believed all that game he was kicking to you, but Pierce is a player. You gave him what he wanted and now he is showing you his true colors. He bagged you. It's just another notch on his belt. It doesn't count if everybody doesn't know about it. He's a jerk, but don't let him see you crying and upset. Get yourself together." She let out a friendly chuckle. The more this girl talked the more familiar she seemed to me. "The way you used to stroll through these halls with your nose up in the air like you was all that is the way you need to walk out of here right now. Others may have gotten the wrong impression and thought you were stuck-up, but I saw it as confidence. Heck, there were times I used to envision me rolling right along with you with the same attitude. So muster up that same confidence and strut right on out of here and forget about Pierce."

I really took this girl's words to heart. "Thanks," I said to her.

"No problem. And if you ever need someone to

talk to," I felt her hand rest on my shoulder, "Just call me, Asia."

When she said my name there was way too much familiarity. I looked up to see none other than Tara Evans standing before me. Obviously she was back from the West Coast where her parents had sent her away to. I nodded and replied, "Thanks, Tara." She gave me a friendly hug and I appreciated the gesture, even though it did not make me feel any less stupid for falling for one of the oldest tricks in the guy book.

"I've got to get to class," Tara said, and then left.

I went into the stall and sat down on the toilet seat. I couldn't go to class. I didn't want to see everyone staring at me. News had definitely gotten around. My name was even scribbled on the insides of the bathroom stall I was sitting in. Apparently I was loose and easy to get with. My feelings were crushed. The boy who I had given my heart to had given me dirt to eat. I couldn't understand why he would do me like that. Why had he chosen me to make a fool of? I had trusted him enough to give him something that I could never get back, and now I was regretting it. In high school, your reputation is everything and mine had now been tarnished.

I heard the bell ring, but I could not force myself to leave my seclusion inside of the girl's bathroom. I did not even come out of the stall. I felt safe and sheltered inside of the bathroom. I did not have to deal with the accusatory stares or the humiliating whispers of the students in school.

Everybody thought they knew what had gone down. They all believed Pierce's side of the story. I could just imagine him bragging to his friends about taking my virginity. He was probably proud that he had gotten me to give it up. He had no clue of the amount of pain he was causing me. My puppy love had turned to hate. What I thought was too good to be true, proved to be just that.

On top of everything, as if to pour salt in my wound, Pierce then had the nerve to play me to the left like I was yesterday's news. He was parading Miranda all over school to let it be known that I was replaced. How could I have been so stupid? I closed my eyes and imagined my daddy. He was my world. He had protected me from stuff like this. I was his princess and he had never wanted me to feel any pain.

I could see his face behind my closed eye lids. I remembered how he would push me on the swings when I was little. I would always jump off and fly through mid air even though I was afraid of heights. Just the thrill of it made me do it every time. It never failed, but I would always land too hard, scrapping my hands and knees just like a little boy. I could still hear my spoiled cries as I looked at my father for comfort. He would give me a reassuring smile, kneel down in front of me, and say, “Shake it off, baby girl.” Just him saying those words would make all of the pain go away. I would stand up, shake it off, and keep on going just to make him proud.

I opened my eyes and whispered, “Shake it off.” Forget Pierce. I wasn’t about to let him beat me. Yes, he had fooled me and I had made a dumb mistake, but he wasn’t about to ruin my entire life. Everybody made mistakes and I was going to shake it off and bounce his lame behind to the left like Mariah Carey’s song says.

I stood up and shook my head from side to side while taking deep breaths. *Forget him,* I told myself. *You didn’t do anything wrong. He did. You don’t have to be embarrassed.* It took me all dang on day to get my courage up, but when school was finally over I walked out of the bathroom and headed for my bus. I walked right pass all of the snickers with my head held high. My confidence faltered momentarily when I saw Pierce standing in his entourage of groupies and teammates. My heart beat sped up ten times, but I kept walking until I stood in front of him.

"Can I talk to you for a minute?" I asked.

Miranda rolled her eyes and answered for him. "No," she seethed. Then she put her hand up to her mouth as if she had made a mistake. "You're stale and old news. I guess you let too many hands go into your cookie jar."

Before I knew it, I hauled off and hit her in her face. Her hands flew up in defense and I hit her one more time just to get out my frustrations. Her nose was bleeding and she was on the ground. Everybody was circled around us while I stomped her out.

"Whoa, Asia, Chill out!" Pierce stated as he pulled me off of Miranda. "Yo, shorty, calm down!"

I spazzed on him too, partially for taking her side and partially for causing me to go through an entire day of torture. "Why did you lie to me?!" I screamed on him.

He chuckled to himself as he grabbed my arm. "You tripping, ma," he said coolly, obviously trying to maintain his image in front of his friends. "You knocked her out, Asia. Maybe I need to keep you on my team."

"Why did you send that text to everybody? You said you loved me! You told me I was special. That was the only reason I even slept with you. I thought you were my man," I said.

Pierce wrapped his arms around my waist and pulled me close to him. He leaned down and tried to push up on me suggestively. "Come on, ma, quit tripping on me. I'll be your boyfriend," he patronized me.

I brought my leg up and kneed him as hard as I could in between his legs. He doubled over in excruciating pain and I was apprehended by the school principal.

"Young lady, what is wrong with you? You need to follow me," he said as he pulled me by the elbow away from the scene of the fight.

If I thought dealing with all of my peers had been tough, things were about to get even tougher.

Chapter Six

I ended up getting kicked out for ten days and Auntie Joy spazzed on me when she had to leave work to pick me up.

"What were you thinking jumping on that girl like that?" She yelled at me all the way through the school parking lot and even louder once we were inside her car. "Now I have to find somebody to watch you while I'm at work."

"I'm almost grown. I don't need a baby sitter," I replied as I rode shotgun in her Honda.

"Almost and being grown are two different things, and don't you forget it."

"But . . ." I started.

"Just be quiet, Asia. I'm not trying to hear a word out of your mouth right now." She shook her head in disgust. "Fighting? What would possess you to fight?"

"Trust me Auntie, if you knew why I did it, you would not blame me," I shot back. "They both deserved it. I'll take these ten days. I ain't tripping."

"Oh you're not tripping?" she mimicked sarcastically. "You listen up and listen good, young lady. I don't care how old you get, you ain't grown until you get out of my house and I don't have to buy the food you eat or the tissue you wipe your little nasty behind with. You just got into high school under my watch and already you are kicked out for fighting. I know these past few months have been rough on you, but you need to slow down and pump your brakes a little. You are a young girl. Stay in a young girl's place. Don't start with this crap. I mean it! I'm not going to tolerate you getting kicked out of school and all."

I fumed silently wishing that I could reveal to her the full story, but I would just be opening up a whole new can of worms if I admitted to having sex, so I didn't respond. Like always, I just let my aunt get her fuss on big time.

"Hello? Do you hear me?" she nagged.

"Yeah," I mumbled.

"Yeah? Girl I know you done lost your mind! I said do you hear me?"

I rolled my eyes because she was on a roll, but I knew better than to say anything other than what I was about to. "Yes ma'am. I hear you, auntie." After that, my aunt did all the talking, or should I say yelling, until we finally made it home.

The rest of the night was silent, but I got a smug satisfaction of beating Miranda down and embarrassing Pierce the same way he had done me. Now that I thought about it, I couldn't believe that I had liked him in the first place. I had put a strain on my friendship with my girl just to be with him and I realized that I owed Tracey an apology.

Since my phone privileges had been taken away, I knew I would have to wait to talk to Tracey until I got back to school. It was going to be a long and boring ten days, but it would give the kids at school time to find a new drama to focus on so that they could take the headlights off of me. There was nothing better than being the 'It Girl' at school, but there was nothing worse than being the girl who was gossiped about. Being an outsider was like death in high school and I hated it. I told myself that I would use my time out of school to get focused and get my head right. I wasn't about to let this little mishap break me.

If I could do things all over again, I would have given Pierce more than a few choice words, but I couldn't, so I had to suck it up, sharpen up my game and make sure that it never happened again. I sure do wish my half brother still went to Cass. He would have put a hurtin' on Pierce for real. I could call him up if I wanted and have him give Pierce the beat down, but then I'd have to tell him why I wanted him to do it, and I was just too ashamed to let my brother in on all the details.

All I knew was that I would never be somebody's puppet again. Pierce had taken advantage of me. I had been in a vulnerable state after losing my father, but never again. I could guarantee that. If anything, I would be the one doing the playing. I wasn't even about to be focused on dudes. They could all kiss my butt for all I cared. Just like Tara had said, high school boys were all the same and I was not about to set myself up to be put in the same situation.

My suspension passed by slowly, and after much sucking up, I finally convinced Auntie Joy to go to work without worrying about me. She could call her watch dog neighbors off from having to watch out for me and come knocking on the door to check to see that I was where I was supposed to be, which was home.

The next morning, Auntie Joy walked into my room to let me know she got called into work early and was getting ready to go.

"Asia, are you asleep?" she asked.

"Not anymore," I replied as I peeked my head from underneath the covers. She gave me that 'Girl, don't go there, this is not the day look' so I checked myself. "I'm up."

"I'm about to go to work. I won't be home until late. I'm pulling a double shift. Don't you even think about leaving this house and I want this place clean from top to bottom," she instructed. "And get up! This ain't no vacation. You are going to wake up every morning just like you are going to school. You can get started on your chores or do some homework or something. I don't want you to get too comfortable. Maybe next time you will think twice before hauling off and punching folks."

"Okay," I said as I lay back down. She leaned over and kissed my forehead then left the room. I got up and followed her to the door while rubbing my eyes sleepily. As soon as I saw her car drive up the block, I raced back to my bedroom and hit the sheets. There was no way I was going to stay up, but as soon as my head caressed the pillow, I heard a knock at the front door.

"I guess the neighbors didn't get the memo," I said to myself. I huffed and puffed in irritation as I stalked back to the front of the house. I put the security chain on the door and opened it slightly so that I could peek out.

"Open the door and let me in," Tracey said. Her brother stood behind her and I closed the door to unhook the chain.

I opened it wide but didn't say anything to Tracey. The day I got suspended I felt as though she had fronted on me. Tara shouldn't have had to show me what was going on with her cell phone. Tracy evidently knew what was going on. She should have pulled me to the side and schooled me on it. Just thinking about it really had me tight. I really did not have anything to say to her at that moment.

"I brought Damian with me. I told him what Pierce did and he's going to handle it for you," Tracey told me.

I crossed my arms across my chest and stood in an offensive stance.

"Can we come in?" Tracey asked snottily. The nerve of this chick.

I stepped to the side and she stormed in. Damian walked in behind her and leaned against the door as he looked down at me. "Are you a'ight?" he asked.

I nodded and looked at my feet nervously. I'd had a crush on him for as long as I could remember, and now he actually seemed concerned.

"Yeah, I'm good," I responded as I motioned for him to walk into the living room.

After closing the door, I turned towards Tracey. She had made herself comfortable on the couch with her shoes kicked off and the remote control in her hand.

"What are you doing here anyway?" I asked. "Ain't you supposed to be in school?"

"Nope," Tracey said. "I'm supposed to be right here. I'm your best friend and I know when you need to be cheered up."

"Tracey, whatever. Don't be fake. You've been acting shady ever since you found out about me and Pierce dating. Now all of a sudden you're acting brand new like we've been good. You treated me just as bad as everybody else did. I thought we were girls when all along you were my biggest hater."

Damian took a seat next to Tracey, took the remote from her hand, and ignored our confrontation completely.

"Asia, I know I've been acting fake lately, but I'm trying to apologize to you. I liked Pierce and I felt like you stole him from me. So yeah, I was hating. But I told myself to get over it because you are my friend and he hurt you. I'm not trying to fall out with you over a boy. We are better than that and I was wrong for tripping on you in the first place. That's why I told Damian to put the dude in his place for you."

I shook my head and replied, "You are my girl. You should have been happy for me instead of being jealous, but I forgive you. Don't let that happen again."

Tracey smirked. "It won't, girl. I swear to God on everything it won't." She cleared her throat and shifted in her seat to get more comfortable. "Now about Pierce . . ."

"Forget Pierce. I'm not thinking about him," I said. "Damian, you don't have to do nothing on my behalf. I think I embarrassed him enough."

He nodded. "Whatever you want Asia. I got you."

I blushed slightly. Tracey noticed it and yelled, "Ugh!"

I punched her in the arm. "Okay, you can go now. I'm about to go back to sleep, and the last thing I need is for Auntie Joy to roll back up in here and catch me having company.

"Uh-uh, I'm chilling over here. I'm skipping school. Ain't no way I'm about to sit up in class another day while you having fun at home."

"Well, I'm going back to sleep. Wake me up in a couple hours," I said as I went back to my room and fell asleep.

I awoke to the smell of food and walked into the kitchen to find Damian cooking.

"Where is Tracey?" I asked while looking around.

He smirked. "She had to go to school. Truancy officer called the crib and busted her out. Granny called her cell phone cussing her out and told her to get her fast butt to school or else."

I burst out laughing. "Ah ha! I'm clowning her. She always talking about her doing whatever she wants and being grown."

"Yeah whatever, she far from grown," he replied as he flipped the omelet he was making in the skillet.

"Why didn't you leave with her?" I asked.

"I was tired. She took the bus because I told her I wasn't leaving until I woke up," he answered nonchalantly.

"You making yourself comfortable ain't you?" I asked sarcastically. I wasn't really bothered by that fact though. I was just acting sassy to get his attention.

"Ya' boy got hungry," he said. "I fixed you one too if that counts."

I smiled. "It counts."

We sat down at the kitchen table and I bit into his homemade omelet. "It's good," I admitted.

"Why did you let ol' boy use you like that?" he asked, changing the subject.

I looked up at him and then lowered my head, almost ashamed. "I didn't know he was a dog. He told me I was special. He lied to me to get what he wanted. I was stupid and I fell for it."

"He didn't lie about you being special, Asia. He's just young and stupid. He took advantage of a great girl. Right now his reputation is all that matters to him. Sleeping with you upgraded his game. The more girls he has sex with, the more popular he becomes. He's a player. It's dumb, but comes with the whole high school thing. I used to be like that too when I was his age."

"That's bull though, because if a girl did the same thing, then she would be called a hoe. It's a double standard," I complained.

"It's life. Girls are expected to have higher standards," Damian said in between bites. "Guys just want to have fun and experiment while they are young."

"That's stupid and y'all don't think about the girls you hurt while you are having fun. Pierce really hurt me. I was a virgin. He took away something that meant something special to me. I thought that I was giving it to someone who cared about me." I couldn't help but let a few tears fall down my face. I wiped them away quickly. "My virginity was the only thing I had that made me different than the other girls. I'm not one of those chicks that will spread her legs for any and everybody. At least I thought I wasn't."

"You're not one of those girls, ma. You're different and you're special. Don't let Pierce take your shine, ma," he stated.

I smiled and finished my breakfast. "Thanks, Damian. I just wish I could have talked to you about Pierce before I gave him some."

He laughed, his Kool-Aid smile warming the features of his face. "You can get at me anytime you need to talk." He grabbed a pen off of the table and wrote his number down on a paper towel. "For real ma, anytime."

He stood to leave and I walked him to the front door. His visit had been unexpected but had made me feel better. I was suddenly glad that Tracey had rudely intruded on my suspension, because if it wasn't for her, I would have never had the conversation with her brother. Once he was gone, I cleaned the house from top to bottom. I didn't want my aunt to know that I had company that day and I did not want to tick her off any more than she already was. I decided to fly straight and make the most of my time off from school, partially to keep auntie happy, but mostly to force myself to move on from my first broken heart.

My suspension basically went the same every day. Tracey tried to stop by when she could, but with the truancy officers involved, her grandma was on her so tough that she couldn't really skip school. To my surprise, Damian came over almost every day. He'd come over as soon as Auntie Joy left for work and I would sleepily get out of bed to let him in. He'd come in and we would crash on the couch for a few hours. He would always wake up first and would make me breakfast to convince me to get out of bed. He was so cool and I could talk to him about anything.

I told him personal things, things that I had

never told anyone and we quickly realized that we had more in common than just his sister. He was quickly becoming a better friend to me than Tracey had ever been. We laughed together, and watched movies together every day. Besides my interactions with Pierce, I had never been so close to a guy as I was with Damian. There was no pressure with him. I didn't have to get cute when he came over. He appreciated me as I was in pajama pants and a baby t-shirt. Once I got used to him coming around, my nervousness faded. He was really my dude and I looked forward to his daily visit. He made me forget about all of the crap that had happened to me at school. As the days passed, I wished he could come back to school with me, to protect me from all of the drama of Cass High. As positive as I tried to think, I knew there was more to come.

Chapter Seven

The day I had been dreading finally arrived. It was time to go back to school. Tracey and Damian picked me up. I could feel Damian looking at me through his rearview mirror, but I had too much on my mind to acknowledge him by looking back. I wondered if the hype concerning Pierce and I had died down, or if the limelight was still on my situation. I knew in just a few more minutes I would find out.

When we pulled up in front of the school, Tracey hopped out and I followed behind her. I looked at Damian as I pulled my book bag from the back seat. He winked and I smiled, remembering all the confidence that he had helped me acquire in such a short time. I waved and walked side by side with

Tracey into the school. Thankfully, everybody seemed to have moved on with their teenage lives. There were no whispers or harsh stares as I made my way to class. I sighed in relief.

"I'm glad that I'm not on everybody's social hit list anymore," I said.

"Girl, you're good. Even if people are still talking, forget them," Tracey replied snidely. I stopped walking when I saw Pierce, but Tracey grabbed my hand. "Girl, come on," she urged.

I let her drag me towards him. Not too long ago I was the one walking Tracey to her classes, and now the tables had been turned. I silently wished that there was another route to my class, but there was no avoiding him. He was standing in my way, so I had to go by him. I took a deep breath, calmed the panic that had built in my heart and put a little umph in my step as I sashayed past him. He didn't say anything to me and I didn't say a word to him, which is how I planned to keep it for the rest of the school year. He was somebody that I would rather not know, and if I did not have to talk to him, I wasn't going to.

It wasn't until about a month later when I was getting ready to head out to school did my world change forever. I had been feeling weird lately and I didn't know what was wrong. I just wasn't myself, and when my auntie walked into my room and asked, "Asia, it's about that time of the month for me, so I know yours is on its way. Do you need any personal items while I'm at the store?"

It was at that exact moment that I realized that my period was late. My mouth dropped in shock and I seemed to tune the world out as I quickly calculated how late it was.

"Asia? Did you hear me?" Auntie Joy asked.

I snapped out of my daze and replied, "Oh yeah, I-I need you to pick me up some," I answered, hoping and praying that my period showed up.

Any other month I would have dreaded those five days of misery, but right now I would have paid for it to come. *How late is it?* I thought. *One week, two, even three?* I couldn't remember, but it really did not matter. I knew that it had not shown up. *Maybe I'm just stressed out and it didn't come because of that. I know I made Pierce use a condom! Or did I? I never really saw him put one on,* I thought frantically. For some reason I couldn't recall if we had used protection or not. It was my first time so I really couldn't tell whether he had one on or not. All I know is that it hurt either way it went.

The room began to spin underneath me. I flopped down on my bed. I needed help, but I knew that I could not tell my aunt what I suspected.

Beep! Beep!

"Asia! Tracey is here!" My aunt shouted. "And didn't I tell you to tell that brother of hers don't be pulling up in front of my house blowing the horn? If Tracey can't walk her tired butt up and knock on the door, then you need to start catching the bus to school again," she fussed. "I don't know why all of a sudden that boy feels the need to chauffer y'all to school anyway.

I knew that Damian was making it a habit of taking us to school now because of me. He was about that drama and I could tell that he wished Pierce would try to start some with me. I had to admit, I was thankful for him.

I raced out of my room, forgetting my book bag on the way. I just had to get out of there. I hopped into the backseat of Damian's car, relief flooding my body as soon as I hit the leather seats. I was silent on the way to school. Tracey's usual chit chat got on my last nerves and I almost went off on her more than once.

When we pulled up to Cass she hopped out. I hesitated.

"Are you coming?" she asked once she realized I wasn't right there behind her.

I shook my head. "No, I don't feel good. I think I'm going to have Damian take me back home. I'm not going to school." I shifted my attention to Damian. "Is that cool with you?"

"Yeah, I'll drop you back off," he answered coolly.

"Okay, call me later," Tracey said before walking away.

I hopped into the front seat and Damian skirted off in the direction of my house.

"I'm not going home," I said. "I need your help. I need to go to a drug store and then a hotel."

He raised his eyebrows, intrigued. "Drug store? A hotel?" I could see his eyebrows arch with excitement.

"Please, Damian. Get your mind out of the gutter. It ain't even like that."

"Why in the world do you need to . . ."

"Please, Damian, don't ask any questions right now. I really need you to do this for me. You are the only person that I can ask. I'm in trouble and you are the only person I trust."

Seeing that I was dead serious, he nodded. "Okay, Asia, I'll help you out." He drove me to the first drug store that we passed.

I ran into Walgreens and got a home pregnancy test. I was ashamed and embarrassed when the store clerk rang up the item. It felt like everybody in line was watching me. Besides, what was a teenage girl doing purchasing a pregnancy test anyway? I wished I wasn't the one who was going through the dilemma, but I put myself at risk when I decided to sleep with Pierce. I was beginning to think that the saying was true. The only way to protect yourself from sex was by not having it at all.

I asked the clerk to double up the bag so that Damian would not be able to see through it. I didn't want him to know yet, because if it turned out that I wasn't pregnant, then I would not tell him what was going on.

We drove to a Holiday Inn, and since he was over eighteen, he got the room. I went in separately so that no one would get suspicious. The last thing I needed was to get caught in the room with Damian.

I rushed into the bathroom and locked it behind me.

Knock, Knock

"Asia, are you a'ight, ma? You're acting kind of weird."

"I'll be out in a minute," I yelled.

I sat down on the toilet seat. My heart was beating out of my chest. I thought I would have a heart attack. My hands fumbled to open the box. I read the instructions and followed them carefully, peeing on the little stick. I was shaking so badly that I made a mess. To make things worse, I had to wait an entire three minutes to get the results. Three minutes felt like thirty, until finally a pale pink strip appeared. I read the box over and over again, but the meaning of the result didn't change.

Pink meant pregnant. I was pregnant.

"Oh my God," I whispered and began to cry. "Damian!"

Damian tried to open the door, but it was still locked and my legs felt like noodles. They were too weak for me to stand and let him in. "Damian!" I cried.

He barreled through the door and picked me up from the floor. His eyes scanned the room until he saw the pregnancy kit.

"Are you?"

"Yeah, I'm pregnant. My life is over," I uttered. "I'm so stupid."

He picked me up from the floor and took me into the room to lie me on the bed. "It's alright, Asia. Everything is going to be alright," he said.

I knew he was just trying to pacify me. There was

no way things were going to be fine. I was in high school and pregnant. My aunt was going to kill me. But sadly, my aunt wasn't the only one I was worried about disappointing. I looked up to the heavens and I softly whispered, "Sorry, Daddy."

Chapter Eight

After taking the test and Damian comforting me a little while, I knew I couldn't stay in that room forever. But I knew that I couldn't go back home either. I needed help in the worst way. Even though I appreciated Damian being there for me, he just couldn't give me the help I needed. I went to the only place that I could think of for help. I went to Ms. Coleman, the high school guidance counselor.

I remembered her friendly face on the first day of school and I knew that she was my only option. I had Damian drop me back off at school. I planned to go straight to Ms. Coleman's office but almost turned around and went another way. Ms. Coleman must have sensed that something was up with me because she called out my name just as I was turning away. As I entered her office Ms. Coleman asked me to take a seat. She sat behind her desk and stared silently at me. I could feel her eyes burning a hole through me, her stare filled with concern. I was afraid. I did not know whether or not my secret would be safe with her, but what other choice did I have.

Over the next few minutes I spilled my guts to Ms. Coleman and her solution was the one I had been trying to avoid. She wanted me to tell my Auntie Joy. After a few minutes of the two of us going back and forth, I reluctantly agreed.

I stood from my seat and took her hand as I wiped my face dry. We walked out of the school hand in hand. I managed to keep dry eyes all the way until we made it out to the school parking lot. By then, my tears were like an unstoppable faucet. Ms. Coleman squeezed my hand reassuringly the entire way to the car.

Ms. Coleman drove to the hospital where my aunt worked and we sat nervously in the hospital waiting room as we waited for the desk nurse to locate my aunt.

Twenty minutes later, Auntie Joy came rushing through the white double doors. "Asia?" she called out frantically. "What's wrong, baby? What's going on?" My aunt was frantic. I guess when she was told that I was at the hospital she thought I might have been hurt or something.

Ms. Coleman stood up and extended her hand. "Hello, my name is Patricia Coleman. I'm Asia's counselor."

Auntie Joy looked from Ms. Coleman to me in confusion. "What happened? Is everything okay?" She grabbed me by the arms and examined me as if she expected to find me bruised up or something. Once she saw that I was physically okay, she released me and gave me a stern look as she said to Ms. Coleman. "Is she in trouble again?" She looked back to me. "Have you been at school fighting like some thug in the streets? I'm telling you, Missy, if you got suspended again . . ."

"Is there somewhere we can sit down and talk?" Ms. Coleman asked, cutting my aunt off.

I looked up and gave Ms. Coleman a "See, I told you look."

Auntie Joy's eyes burned a hole through me, but I never looked up at her. I couldn't. I was too ashamed.

"Yeah we can go to the cafeteria," Auntie said as she led the way. Ms. Coleman ordered a cup of coffee for herself after my auntie and I declined her offer for anything. Then we all sat down.

"Look, I know you are on the clock, so we won't waste your time beating around the bush." Ms. Coleman looked at me. "Asia has something she wants to tell you," Ms. Coleman began. "I urge you to please hear her out and keep in mind that she is young and is probably terrified right now."

"Will you quit talking in circles and tell me what is going on?" Auntie Joy exclaimed.

I was silent.

"Asia!" Auntie Joy yelled.

"I'm pregnant," I whispered.

"You're what?" Auntie Joy said as she stood up. Her anger put fear in my heart. "I have warned you time and time again about being fast, about growing up too quickly."

"Please, could you just sit down," Ms. Coleman said, noticing all eyes were on us due to my aunt's outburst.

I couldn't even respond. All I could do was cry. In fact, I bawled as Ms. Coleman rubbed my back in an effort to calm me down.

"I think we all should calm down. Asia is in a serious situation and we need to think about the options," Ms. Coleman stated.

"The options? We? This is Asia's problem," my aunt told Ms. Coleman. "Unless you are going to let her come and live with you, there is no we. She wanted to be grown, so now she is grown. I'm not spending my hard earned money on no abortion, or no nappy headed baby that I did not birth. She is on her own. She needs to get a job and she needs to clean up her own mess, because I'm done."

"I'm sorry," I said.

"You sure are," Auntie Joy replied. "I have to get back to work. Asia, you have three months to get a job and find a place to stay. I told you before you got yourself into this. This is your problem, not mine."

And just like that, I was on my own.

Chapter Nine

Ms. Coleman stood and took my hand. "You know what?" she said to my aunt Joy before she could stomp all the way off. "Everyone makes mistakes. Asia doesn't need your ridicule. She's only a child. She needs your support. This is how we lose our young, black girls to the system, by making them feel that no one is supporting them. She's not asking you to raise her baby. She's just asking you for your support."

"Well she does not have it," my aunt turned and snapped as she walked back towards the table. "When her father died, I took her in and this is how she repays me." Auntie Joy sneered at me and then turned her back on me. I knew that our relationship would never be the same. Ms. Coleman knew that no matter what she said at this point, my aunt's mind was made up.

Ms. Coleman and I walked out of the hospital together. I was distraught and did not know what to do. It was clear that Auntie Joy was not going to stand in my corner for this, but I wasn't strong enough to face this alone.

"What am I going to do? I'm all alone. I don't have anywhere to turn," I said. I looked at Ms. Coleman and could see tears building in her eyes. She gave me a smile and a pat on the hand.

"You are not alone, Asia. You have me. We will go and get your things from your aunt's. You can stay with me until we figure this out," Ms. Coleman stated. "You don't need the stress of her ranting and raving right now. From the sounds of it, your aunt isn't going to have a problem with you coming to stay with me for a while."

I was quiet, not because I didn't have much to say, but because I didn't know what to say first. I wanted to apologize to her for getting her involved in my problems, and to ask her why she was being so nice, but I couldn't find the words. Instead, I sat in her passenger seat and rode in silence while my mind tried to wrap itself around upcoming motherhood.

We went to pack my things, and just as she promised, she welcomed me into her home. She lived in a three bedroom ranch style home just outside of Detroit. It was nice with a quaint lawn and two car garage. Her taste was elaborate and her home chic. I was impressed.

"Come on in and make yourself comfortable," she invited. "You can take the bedroom down the hall on the left."

"Thank you." My voice was so genuine and full of emotion. I was grateful for her help, but I still did not know how long it was going to last.

"While you unpack, I'm going to make some calls and find you a good doctor. We have to figure out how far along you are."

I nodded and retreated to the comfortable space that had become mine.

Ms. Coleman was able to get me into the doctor's office the next afternoon. Ms. Coleman was kind enough to write me an excuse from class and take me on her lunch break. We walked into the doctor's office and I checked in with the receptionist. I was so afraid. All that morning I had been experiencing crazy morning sickness, and it seemed like ever since I confirmed that I was pregnant, my body felt weird all over. I didn't want to be there. I was ashamed and did not know what to expect.

Ms. Coleman said that the next couple of days she would take me to do all the things that I needed to do to get the ball rolling with my pregnancy. The next day, after school, she'd scheduled me an appointment at the WIC offices so that I could sign up for the things that they give expectant mothers. She also planned to take me to the social service office so that I could sign up for healthcare for me and my baby.

Just in case I did decide to go all the way through with this pregnancy, I was relieved to know that there were State programs that would help me get through this. I never pictured myself as one of those ghetto chicks who got stuck on welfare, but here I was. I had a belly full of baby and my hand out waiting for some government assistance. I couldn't help but think if my daddy was alive my life would have never gone down this path.

"Asia Smith!"

I jumped when my name was called by the nurse.

"It's okay," Ms. Coleman whispered. "I'm right here with you."

I got up and followed the nurse into the examination room. I felt like I had to throw up when I saw the bed and metal contraptions that were on the counter beside the bed. "What is all of this?" I asked.

The doctor entered the room smiling warmly. She was an older black woman who wore a white lab jacket. "Hello, Asia. I'm Dr. Neely. I will be your doctor throughout the length of your pregnancy." She held out her hand to me and I shook it. Her hands were warm and soft, while her touch was motherly and comforting. "I take it you have never had a pap smear or vaginal exam before?"

"A pap say what?" I asked.

Ms. Coleman and Dr. Neely laughed lightly. The nurse chuckled as well as she exited the room, leaving the doctor to tend to her business with me.

"Don't worry, Asia. I am going to take good care of you and your baby. I've been doing this for a very long time," Dr. Neely assured. "As a matter of fact, I've been taking care of Ms. Coleman here for a very long time as well." She looked up at Ms. Coleman and smiled, then turned her attention back towards me. "Ms. Coleman and I are going to go in the hallway and talk while you get undressed. When you are done, lie on the table and put your feet in the stirrups."

I nodded, and when they walked out, I followed

her instructions. Minutes later they were back. Ms. Coleman stood at the head of the bed, holding my hand and Dr. Neely took a seat between my legs. I instinctively closed them to shield her from seeing my private areas.

"I'm going to open your legs and give you an exam. I will have to put my hands down there, okay?" the doctor informed me.

"Okay," I responded. I took a deep breath to calm down. Just the fact that she was explaining things to me step by step made it easier. I was glad that Ms. Coleman had chosen Dr. Neely. My body tensed and I cringed in pain as she put different tools and instruments in places that I felt they shouldn't be.

"How often do you have sex, Asia?" the doctor asked while she examined me.

"I don't. I-I mean, I've only done it once," I replied.

"Okay, well this may hurt a bit, so tell me if it hurts too badly and we'll stop okay?"

"Okay."

She fiddled around some more for about one or two minutes, and when she was done, I sighed in relief. She then brought a monitor over to my bed-side. She put some warm gel on my stomach and put what looked like a microscope on my stomach. A steady beat filled the room and I saw a tiny spot of white on the screen that was beside the bed up near my head.

"This is your baby and that sound that you are hearing is your baby's heartbeat," Dr. Neely explained. I was afraid, but I smiled at the calm rhythm.

"How far along is she?" Ms. Coleman asked.

"I would say nine weeks," Dr. Neely confirmed. "So you have seven months ahead of you."

Ms. Coleman and I looked at each other. She smiled and so did I, although I wasn't happy about having a baby. I wanted to talk to Ms. Coleman about an abortion, but I did not know how to tell her. After getting an ultrasound printed, I left the doctor with a new prescription for prenatal vitamins.

"Ms. Coleman, I want to thank you for letting me stay with you," I said as she drove us back to the school. "I know you did not have to do everything you just did, going to the doctors with me and all. As a matter of fact, I really shouldn't have even been in there," I stated.

"Why not?"

"I think I want an abortion," I blurted out quickly.

Ms. Coleman brought the car to a stop in the middle of the road. "Oh, Asia. You have been blessed with something special. Have you thought about this?"

"I just don't want a baby. I'm too young and I can't take care of a baby. I'm just not ready," I admitted. "I hate to say it, but my auntie is right; she's been right all along. I should have listened to her."

"I know how you feel," Ms. Coleman started until I cut her off.

"All adults say that, Ms. Coleman, but you can't possibly . . ."

Now it was her turn to cut me off.

"When I was in high school I had an abortion," she confessed. "I was just like you. I was so afraid to tell my mother that I went to an unlicensed clinic. The abortion worked, but it was done incorrectly and robbed me of the ability to ever have children. Don't make the same mistake I made, Asia. Please be sure about this. There are a million women like me who would love to be in your shoes. I will even help you with your baby. You can stay with me as long as you need to."

"I don't have anyone. I don't want my baby to not have anyone."

"What if I told you that I wanted to adopt your

baby, Asia? If you are dead set on not wanting to be a mother, I would be honored to raise your baby."

"You would do that for me?" I asked. The thought of giving my baby up for adoption had crossed my mind. I thought about giving my child up and selfishly it seemed like a great solution to my problem. No matter what way I looked at it, I did not want a baby, and if I could make Ms. Coleman's life more complete by giving up my baby to her, then I was willing to do it. I could go back to being a regular teenager and I wouldn't feel guilty about killing an innocent life. I knew that any child would be lucky to have Ms. Coleman for a mother.

"Asia, you would be giving me a blessing. I would be honored to be a mother to that child growing inside of you," she said.

I leaned over and hugged her tightly. "Thank you." I looked out of the window up at the sky and silently thanked God too. Ms. Coleman had been right about what she'd said before, God did have a plan.

"No, thank you, Asia." Ms Coleman smiled the entire way back to Cass.

Ms. Coleman and I thought it would be better if no one knew about my pregnancy. I was home schooled for the next seven months. The only other person who knew about it was Damian, and he promised not to tell Tracey about it. He came to see me faithfully, refusing to give up our friendship just because I was knocked up. I didn't even tell Pierce. It wasn't his decision to make, and when I was asked who the father of my child was, I always said that I did not know. I didn't want there to be any issues when it came time for Ms. Coleman to adopt the baby and for me to relinquish my parental rights.

My Auntie Joy didn't put up a fight in allowing me to stay with Ms. Coleman. She was glad to wash her hands of the situation. Ms. Coleman and I grew close, but it still didn't fill the void of not having my blood there for me. She helped me deal with the changes that my body was going through, and believe me, it went through a LOT of changes.

My breasts swelled two times their normal size and they were sore all the time. Even the steady beat from the shower head was too intense for the sensitive melons that my breasts had become. To make matters worse, they leaked. Can you say NASTY! I was so disgusted with myself. My nose spread, which made me look like a monkey, and it seemed like I picked up another pound every single day. Ms. Coleman thought I glowed. I told her that I sweated. She would laugh when I would complain, but she helped me through every single step of the way.

I knew that my body was going through something that it was not prepared to endure. I was a baby myself, a baby having a baby. The only good thing that had come out of it was that my hair was growing like crazy. I was always tired and there was nothing attractive, or fun, about being the size of a baby whale. I looked at my Auntie Joy letting me stay with Ms. Coleman as a double plus, because I was probably too big to even fit in my aunts little house any more.

My aunt and I didn't really speak much after that day in the hospital. I called and told her what Ms. Coleman and I planned to do, but she never invited me to come back home, so I never asked her if I could. I was happy with Ms. Coleman. She treated me with respect and she taught me more things in those seven months about being a woman than I had learned my entire life.

I regretted having sex with Pierce. That one night of passion, that was not passionate at all, was not worth the lifetime of pain that I had created for myself. I should have told him no. I was young and free, with the entire world ahead of me. I jeopardized that by giving myself to someone who wasn't my husband. I thought about all of the other young girls who didn't have a Ms. Coleman to bail them out of teenage pregnancy. I was very fortunate to have her in my life. A woman like her was a blessing. I knew that she would give my baby (well, her baby) everything that I could not. She was going to be a great mother. I wished that I could have grown up with one in my life just like her.

I felt cut off and shielded from the world, but I knew that it was how it had to be unless I wanted to explain my protruding belly. I told Tracey that I had moved out of town to attend a performing arts academy for the remainder of the year and Damian kept his promise to me. He was a really great guy and he sometimes made references about me being his girlfriend, but I wasn't ready for all of that. I was still carrying a baby by my supposed first boyfriend. I was still in high school and was already over teenage relationships. He respected and understood how I felt, so we remained close friends. Surprisingly he was with me all the way until the end.

On August 14, 2009, I was studying with Damian while Ms. Coleman made us all dinner in the kitchen. All of a sudden I felt the sudden urge to pee. When I stood up a gush of water flowed from between my thighs.

"Oh my GOD! I think my water broke!" I announced loudly as my eyes bugged out.

"Ms. Coleman! Her water broke!" Damian screamed as he put his hand on the small of my back and sat me back down in the chair.

Ms. Coleman rushed into the room. When she saw the panic in my eyes, she set into motion. "Okay Damian, go and get the overnight bag from the nursery. I'll call Dr. Neely and let her know we are on our way. Asia, sit tight sweetheart. Are you in pain?"

I shook my head and replied, "No, it doesn't hurt, but it don't feel good. There is like a lot of pressure down there."

Ms. Coleman placed the call and minutes later we were out the door. She drove swiftly but cautiously to the hospital and had Damian go and park the car while we went directly into emergency.

I was wheeled up to the maternity ward. As soon as the elevator doors opened I saw Dr. Neely's smiling face.

"Are you ready for this?" she asked.

"No," I said honestly.

"Well, that baby is coming, so you better get ready," she said excitedly. It was almost as if she was about to become a mother herself.

I had been trying to mentally prepare myself for the labor. I had been reading up on it and I had discovered that every woman had a different experience when it came to giving birth. The one thing I feared the most was the pain, and I was beginning to feel contractions already.

Just as I was being escorted into the birthing center, Damian emerged from the elevators.

"Wait!" he yelled. He approached us and asked, "Can I come too? I want to be here for Asia."

Ms. Coleman looked at me and I nodded. I was sweating profusely and breathing deeply. At that moment I didn't care who came into the room with me, as long as they got me in there. I was so ready to have this baby that I didn't know what to do.

"Okay, let's rock and roll. We have to get you an epidural quickly. You're too young to take this naturally. We don't want your body to go into shock."

Dr. Neely exited the room and then came back with a couple of other people. One explained that he would be injecting the epidural and, shortly after, he produced one of the biggest needles I had ever seen in my life. I closed my eyes as it penetrated my skin.

"Oww!" I yelled angrily.

"Don't worry, you won't be able to feel anything in a minute," Ms. Coleman said.

Moments later my entire bottom half felt numb, but I could still feel the pressure. It made me feel like I wanted to push. My body was tired, weak, and uncomfortable. Those contractions literally felt like they were ripping my little butt apart, but Damian and Ms. Coleman were right by my side. I yelled at them, and cussed them out the entire time, but they never left. They were stuck to me like glue. I appreciated them because I knew that I could have never done this alone.

After seven hours and twenty minutes of labor, I was relieved to hear the screeching screams of a baby.

"It's a boy!" Dr. Neely announced. "It's a beautiful, healthy, baby boy!"

I looked up and took one look at the wrinkled, slimy baby, then collapsed from exhaustion.

I awoke a couple of hours later. I hurt everywhere, but the sight before me brought tears to my

Ms. Coleman sat at my bedside with the baby er arms and Damian was knocked out in the ner chair.

'Is he okay?" I whispered. My throat and lips ere dry. Ms. Coleman stood and handed me the baby. She then grabbed a cup of water and put it to my lips. I gratefully sipped it.

"He is more than okay, Asia. He's beautiful. He's your son if you want him to be," she said with tears of joy in her eyes.

I admired the baby in my arms. He was so tiny and he looked just like me. His skin was the same color and tone as mine. He had my eyes and nose. He was my baby, but I knew that I could never give him the life that he deserved. I was way too young. He was a mistake that I wasn't ready to handle. I had to think about him and do what was best for him.

"No, he is your baby, Ms. Coleman. I want you to have him. I know that you will love him and take care of him, the same way you did for his mother." I smiled. "I trust you."

Ms. Coleman leaned over and kissed me on the forehead. "Asia, I would like for you to be a part of my family. I know you don't have anywhere to go. You would make a great big sister to him."

"Big sister?"

Ms. Coleman nodded. "I want to adopt you both. That way you can still be a part of his life. He will be my son, but you will be my daughter as well. We'll be family."

Tears flowed down my face. She did not know how much she had blessed my life in such a short period of time. I was supposed to be another black statistic, a teenage mother. I had made the mistake of having premarital sex at a young age. It was something that I wished I could take back, but the deed was done. The baby was here and I couldn't take it back, but I could live right from now on. I could learn from my mistakes and be a great daughter to Ms. Coleman and a great sister to this baby.

"I would love to be his sister. Thank you, Ms. Coleman," I said between sobs.

"You are more than welcome, Asia, and when you are ready, you can start calling me Mom," she said.

"What do you want to name him?" she asked.

"I get to name him?" I could not believe she was giving me the privilege.

"Why not? I think you deserve to do at least that," she said.

I looked at Damian who was sleeping in the corner and I smiled. He was such a great friend. He had stood by my side and kept secrets that others would have told. I knew that once I got myself together that he would be my boyfriend, but for now, he was my inspiration.

"Damian Coleman."

Ms. Coleman, I mean my new mom looked back at Damian and smiled. "That's a fine name."

In a couple of weeks, just as she'd promised, Ms. Coleman held out the adoption papers for me and little Damian. I signed without hesitation on the dotted line. I was happy that she had rescued me from the perils of teenage motherhood and I vowed that I would never lose my focus again. Sex was for grown, married women and I was not that. I decided then and there to make my new mom proud and slow down to enjoy being me, an immature, carefree, teenager that was focused on things that girls my age focused on. I had learned my lesson. I just hoped that all the other young, black girls out there would not have to go through what I went through to know that the best form of protected sex is no sex at all.